The
Russian
In The
Attic

Marcey Goulder Forman

Winston-Derek Publishers, Inc.
Pennywell Drive—P.O. Box 90883
Nashville, TN 37209

PUBLISHED BY WINSTON-DEREK PUBLISHERS, INC.
Nashville, Tennessee 37205

Library of Congress Catalog Card No: 88-50755
ISBN: 1-55523--160-8

Printed in the United States of America

Dedication

This book is for Jacqueline, Jessica, and Rick.
I also dedicate it to the memory of Samantha Smith.

Contents

Chapter One

The boy was running. He was running as hard and as fast as he could. He dodged around groups of people, many with young children. He glanced back over his shoulder to see if the men were still following him. Yes, they were. There were two men, one short and fat with a bald head who perspired a lot; the boy remembered how the man's sweat smelled in the early spring heat. The other man was tall with a ruddy complexion and small, mean eyes. The boy slammed into someone while he was looking backwards. It was a little girl about six years old. Her popcorn spilled on the red cement.

"Sorry," the boy muttered as she burst into tears. He felt bad about it, but he didn't stop running. The men were getting closer.

The boy's name was Mikhail Petrovitch Lermantov, and he was scared. He half wished he could turn around and go back, say I'm sorry to the men who followed him, and be forgiven. But he knew he could not. If he did, he feared he would be punished. He was a Russian boy, and he might be punished in a way most American children couldn't imagine. Perhaps he would be sent to a work camp or to an isolated village in Siberia, like his aunt.

So Mikhail continued to run. He passed rows of gaily colored buildings painted like tiny Swiss cottages. He passed eight-foot-tall figures of Huckleberry Hound and Yogi Bear. He passed shops selling souvenirs and Belgian waffles, a delicacy he'd never known until today. Mikhail heard the clatter of the giant rollercoaster known as The Beast and the delighted screams of dozens of children as a huge pirate ship rocked end to end, threatening to spill them out but never quite doing so. Mikhail loved King's Island Amusement Park, but he had to get out—and this might be his only chance.

Suddenly, Mikhail spotted a young man dressed in white. He was sweeping tiny bits of trash into his long-handled dust pan. Then he opened an unmarked door in a large brick building and disappeared inside.

Mikhail glanced back again. A mob of families blocked his view of his pursuers. If Mikhail couldn't see the men, then the men couldn't see him. Good. He dashed after the dust-pan man. Panting, he let himself into a cool hallway. He longed to stand there and catch his breath, but he didn't dare. Any delay might mean his pursuers would catch him.

The dust-pan man was walking toward a red exit sign at the end of the hall. But Mikhail wasn't ready to go outside yet. A heavy door was on his right. Cautiously, he opened it. It was a stairway. He took the stairs two at a time. All the time his heart was pounding so loudly that he wondered if unseen people in the building could hear it. When he got to the top, Mikhail was in another hall with many doors. Halfway down, a door stood open. Mikhail peered around the corner. It was a conference room with a big table and many chairs. It was empty. He entered, walked over to the large windows and looked out. Mikhail realized he was directly over the entrance to the amusement park. The part of the building he was in was built like a bridge across the wide entrance. Families hurried in or strolled out. Then he spotted a familiar face. It was the tall man. Just then a small child released a helium balloon. The bright yellow balloon floated upwards toward his window. The big man's eye followed it. Mikhail jumped back behind the curtain. He couldn't let the man see him!

A few moments later, when Mikhail peeked outside again, the man's eyes were elsewhere. He was turning around in a circle and looking carefully at all the boys who passed. But where was his partner? What if the fat man were climbing the stairs of Mikhail's building even now? Any minute he might be caught.

Mikhail thought of crawling under a corner

desk until the park closed. But he knew the plan was no good. The men chasing him were very thorough. They would search every room and look under every desk. If necessary, they would recruit the security guides to help them. They would apologize that they had lost their nephew, and could the guides help them hunt for a twelve-year-old boy, about so high, with gray eyes and blond hair? The guides were used to looking for lost children, so of course they would. They would have no idea that the men were not his uncles or that they might hurt him.

Mikhail thought of his father, and for a moment tears came to his eyes. But he bit his lip and made the tears go away. Crying was for babies, and if Mikhail was to start a new life, he must act like a man.

Mikhail carefully looked down the hall. It was empty. He ran toward the far exit sign and hurried down the stairs. He paused at the bottom and opened the door very slowly, only a crack. A woman was coming down the hall toward him. He shut the door and turned. Another, heavier door was set in the wall behind him. This door had a window. It looked out into a narrow wooden walk-way between two buildings. Mikhail ran outside. He followed the wooden path.

"Hey!" someone shouted. Mikhail heard heavy footsteps pound hollowly behind him. He didn't

bother to turn. He didn't have time. If the footsteps belonged to one of the two men, he had to
escape. If it wasn't, it still didn't matter because a
park employee who captured him would broadcast
an appeal to relatives. Then the men would grab
him.

Mikhail darted around another building toward
a small wooden fence with a handle. He turned
the handle and let himself inside. He wrinkled his
nose. It smelled nasty. Mikhail was in the garbage
area. The footsteps ran past, then faded.

All was silence. Silence and smell. Mikhail
smelled the remains of hamburgers and cigarettes
and leftover soda pop. He told himself he didn't
mind the stink if it meant that he could be safe.
Abruptly he heard a buzzing. Several angry yellow
jackets dive-bombed his head. Mikhail hated bees.
He didn't want to get stung, but he told himself he
would take a hundred stings rather than be
caught by the two men. Then Mikhail realized
even one sting would hurt, and hurt so bad it
might make him yell. His yell could bring the two
men. He couldn't get caught, not this close to freedom!

Mikhail pressed his cheek against two wooden
slats and looked between them. He saw no one.
Once again he let himself out. Which way was the
main entrance? He was hopelessly lost, but decided going somewhere was better than standing

still. Only if he moved could he find his way out. He started to walk, and he walked for what seemed like a long time. The path snaked through enclosed courtyards and around buildings. Finally, he came to a wooden fence with a closed door. When he opened the door, Mikhail found himself in the parking lot. As he shut the door, he noticed a sign on the side facing the cars. "Employees Only" it said. Good. Most likely the men wouldn't think of looking here.

The sun glinted on car windows. The colors dazzled him, and he blinked. So many cars! All the cars in America surely must be in this lot! At home in Moscow only Party officials or famous comrades drove cars. But here cars were everywhere, and even families drove them . . . so many families. Mikhail figured that either most people could afford cars because they were cheap, or else most people in America were rich. But at home, political officers said Americans were poor and hungry. Wouldn't hungry people buy food before they would buy cars? It didn't make sense. A lot of things didn't make sense. That's why Mikhail was running. He wanted answers.

Mikhail walked to his right, toward the main entrance. Now that he was out of the park, he wasn't sure where he wanted to go, but he knew he had to get away. He decided he could be spotted too easily walking along the fence, so he cut between the cars and began to zig zag through the rows. When he judged he was closer to the huge sign at the end of the lot than he was to the main entrance, he stopped. Very shortly, he found what he was looking for. It was a car with the driver's window rolled part way down. The driver, apparently wanting to keep the car from getting too hot, left the window open, but not open so far that an adult could reach inside and unlock the door. Mikhail, however, was no adult. His arms were skinny. He reached inside. He found that by standing on his tiptoes and leaning, he could just barely grasp the knob that locked the door. He held his breath and stretched . . .there! With the tips of his fingers he pulled the knob up. Then he sighed and rubbed his arm.

Mikhail opened the door and crawled into the back—and there was a blanket thrown in a heap on the floor. It was early April, but it felt more like late June thanks to a heat wave. Despite the warm temperature, he crawled under the blanket. He bunched himself into the smallest ball possible and hoped no one would look under the blanket. He also hoped the car's owners would come back soon. It was hot under there.

He must have fallen asleep. The next thing he knew, someone was sticking a key in the lock. He heard voices. He held his breath and hoped no one would climb on top of him. He clutched a lucky kopeck in his pocket. His luck held. Two people got in front and only one got in the back seat, and that person got in on the other side.

"Well, I liked the racing coasters the best. It was really neat racing with people in another roller coaster right beside us. I loved going so fast," said a child in the back seat. It sounded like a girl.

"Hah! If you thought it was so neat, why did you scream the whole time, then throw up when you got out?" retorted an older boy from the front seat.

"I wasn't scared," the girl insisted. "I just threw up from eating too much cotton candy. I told you it was too sweet."

"Children, that's enough," said the woman in the driver's seat. "We've had a wonderful day, now don't spoil it by arguing." She turned the key and Mikhail heard the engine jump to life. Slowly, the car began to back up. When Mikhail felt the car stop, he was afraid he'd been discovered. But the woman was simply shifting gears. The car began to move forward again.

"Do you kids want to stop for supper on the way home, or just drive straight through?"

"Ugh, don't mention food," the girl groaned.

"Mom, I really want to get back. I promised Steve I'd play basketball with him tonight."

Mikhail felt the car stop, then make a right

turn. When the car started again, it began to go a lot faster.

"Once we get on the freeway, it won't take long," the woman said. "We should be home in a little over an hour."

"Yeah," the boy laughed, "provided you don't get pulled over by a cop again!"

"Scott, that's enough! I'm a good driver. Besides, it only happened once."

The boy laughed. Mikhail heard a sharp click, followed by a burst of loud music. "Mind if I listen to some rock?"

"Only if you keep it down," the girl said. "I want to go to sleep."

The music got softer. The girl lay down on the seat. Mikhail heard her soft breathing near his ear. He tried to breathe through his mouth, so she wouldn't hear him. It was dark and warm under the blanket. The rhythm of the car traveling at a constant speed was monotonous. It rocked them both to sleep.

Chapter Two

The car's stopping jarred Mikhail awake. For a frightening moment he couldn't recall where he was. The car moved again and Mikhail remembered. It turned and continued at a much slower rate than on the freeway. Mikhail decided that the family would probably be home soon. How was he going to get out of the car without them discovering him? Should he let them find him and, perhaps, turn him in? Should he announce himself and beg for help? They might be angry if they found a stowaway in the back; maybe he should let them know he was hiding in the back seat. But somehow, he couldn't bring himself to sit up and say, "I hope you don't mind, but I'm running away from home and want your help." The mother might be angry. He couldn't face another angry adult that day. He decided to start with the girl.

Very slowly, he lifted the edge of the blanket and looked out. He was inches away from the girl. Her eyes were shut and her long blonde hair tumbled over her face. She looked about his age. He pulled the blanket down over his shoulders, then cautiously touched her cheek. What if she woke up and screamed when she saw him? Her mother might be startled and jerk the wheel of the car. They could have an accident. If people were hurt, the Americans might deport him. He'd be sent back to Russia, and authorities there would probably send him to Siberia.

But the girl didn't move. Mikhail stared at her in confusion. He decided he couldn't stay on the floor of the car forever. He had to do something.

Gently he touched the girl's cheek again. Her lashes fluttered and her eyes opened. They were very big and very brown. She gasped. Mikhail quickly put his finger across his lips. He silently pleaded with her not to scream.

She didn't. She looked at him in wonder.

He risked a whisper. "I'm running away and I need to hide. Will you help me?"

The girl smiled and studied his face. What she saw in it must have satisfied her, because she nodded. She, too, put her finger over her lips and hissed, "Shh." Then she sat up and said, "Are we almost home?"

"Are you awake, darling? Feeling better? We should be there in five minutes," the mother said.

"Lisa, can I turn the music up, now that you're awake?" Scott asked.

"Sure," Lisa said.

"Not too loud," their mother cautioned. "I value my eardrums."

Lisa lay back down on the seat and whispered

11

to Mikhail, "Make yourself as small as you can and don't move. Don't get out of the car until I come back for you, okay?" Then she draped the blanket over his body, tugging it here and there to make sure he was completely hidden.

The car made another turn, slowed, then stopped.

"Everybody out," the mother said.

Lisa scooted to her mother's side of the car. "I've changed my mind, Mom. I think I want supper. When will Ben be home?"

"What are you, a walking appetite?" asked Scott as he slammed the door shut.

Their mother ignored him. "Ben is working late, and he said he'd grab something on the way home. I can make you a hamburger now, if you'd like."

Lisa shut her door, and Mikhail heard their voices growing fainter as they entered the house. "Yes, please," she said.

"There's some potato salad left. Want some of that?"

"And a cookie," Lisa said.

"Nothing but appetite," muttered Scott.

Mikhail was left alone in the car. He pulled the blanket off and peeked out a window. He was in the garage. He could see a lawnmower and two bicycles along one wall. A shovel and a rake were hung on pegs on another wall. He thought of getting out of the car and hiding in a corner of the garage, but there was nowhere else to hide. So he waited for Lisa in the car.

He didn't have to wait long. When the door to the house opened and a shaft of light spilled out, Mikhail ducked his head behind the seat.

"It's okay," Lisa said softly. "It's only me."

He looked up. Her nose was pressed against the window looking at him.

"You can get out now. Bring the blanket."

Obediently, Mikhail pushed the seat forward and climbed out. It felt good to stretch his legs after lying in a cramped position for so long.

"Thank you," he said. "I really . . ."

"Don't talk here," said Lisa quietly. "Mom or Scott might hear us. Come on."

She walked to a far corner of the garage and yanked a chain suspended from the ceiling. Mikhail looked up. A square of wood was set into the ceiling. As Lisa yanked, the square opened, and a set of rough wooden steps came down. She started to climb, and motioned that he follow.

Mikhail put his hands on the floor to heave himself over the edge and into the hiding place. The floor was dusty. Lisa was sitting cross-legged, waiting for him. As he sat down beside her, she grabbed a handle and pulled. The stairs followed them up and the door shut. It was gloomy, but only for a moment. Then a light appeared.

13

"Flashlight," Lisa explained. "We always leave it by the stairs so we can find our way to the wall switch."

She stood up, and Mikhail watched the circle of light move over to a wall near a window. Lisa pulled the shade down, then she flipped a switch. An overhead light came on. "That's better," she said.

Mikhail looked around curiously. The room was large, apparently the size of the two-car garage below them. It was cluttered with suitcases, trunks, a rack with garment bags hanging from it, a large doll house, a tricycle, a collapsed crib and high chair, and half a dozen large cardboard boxes. Mikhail stood up and followed Lisa behind the boxes. There he saw an old couch, a table with a lamp on it, and a scarred wooden dinette table with three chairs. One of the chairs was missing a slat across the back.

Lisa gestured. "We store junk here. A couple years ago Scott and I decided to make this a sort of club house for us and our friends. So Mom moved some worn-out furniture up here. Nobody really uses this place anymore, except as storage." She turned and studied his face. "Who are you? What's going on?"

Mikhail hesitated. She was offering him this wonderful hiding place. She hadn't given him away to her family. But he wasn't in the habit of trusting people. Not completely.

"My name is Ivan Petrovitch Belkin."

Lisa's eyes got very round. "Are you a communist?" she asked.

He shook his head. "No. My father is. I am too young to be a Party member. I am running away."

Lisa sat down on the couch. "From Russia? How on earth did you get here?"

"Where are we?" he asked.

"Columbus, Ohio."

He decided to trust her with *some* of the truth. After all, he had to trust someone. "I was in Cincinnati," he said. "The Russian government has an embassy in Washington and consulates in San Francisco and New York. The Americans agreed we could open another consulate in Cincinnati."

"What's a consulate?"

"It is a trade and information office. It's used by people in America who want to know something about the Soviet Union, or want to sell wheat to Russia or buy furs. These people can talk to someone who represents the government."

"Why don't they talk to the ambassador?" Lisa asked.

"The ambassador is busy with other duties, like talking to the president."

"So what were you doing in Cincinnati?"

Mikhail sat down beside her. He ran his hand

over the tan corduroy of the seat. It felt good. "My father was an officer with the embassy in Washington. He was sent to Cincinnati for three days to help open the consulate and to hold a news conference to tell people about the new consulate and about the wonderful trade opportunities with the Union of Soviet Socialist Republics."

"And he took you to King's Island," Lisa stated, "and you ran away."

Mikhail sighed. "Not exactly."

"Lisa. Lee-sah. Where are you?" a voice called in the distance.

Lisa jumped up. "Supper! I almost forgot! Stay here. I'll be right back." She ran to the stairs and shoved them. They stretched themselves down into the garage and she hurried down. "Coming, Mom," she shouted.

Supper. It sounded so tempting. It had been hours since Mikhail had eaten more than cotton candy. Nevertheless, he grimly forced the thought from his mind. It might be hours before he'd eat again. Better not think about food.

A few minutes later he heard someone coming up the stairs. Hastily, Mikhail ducked behind a big trunk. He heard the creak of the stairs being pulled into place, then Lisa said, "It's okay, Ivan. It's just me. I didn't mean to scare you. I brought you some food."

When he dusted his knees off and came out, he

16

saw she had put a plate on the table. Lisa pulled a can of soda pop from one pocket of her jeans and a napkin from another.

"Come eat," she invited.

His mouth watered. "Where's yours?" he asked.

She grinned. "I wasn't hungry. Not after all that food today! I just pretended I was so I could bring you some supper. Do you like hamburgers?"

Chapter Three

The hamburger was hot, and the juice ran down his chin. It was slightly pink in the middle, the way he liked it. The potato salad was cold, with large chunks of potatoes coated with a blend of mustard and mayonnaise. Inside the napkin was a large chocolate chip cookie. The supper was perfect. He chewed and swallowed several mouthfuls of food before he remembered his manners.

"Your mother is a very delicious cook, and you are very kind to bring me this food," he said.

Lisa pulled an apple from her pocket. "I'll munch on this while you eat. Tell me the rest of your story."

"My father and I have been in America since I was six. We came over right after my mother died. My father is a very well-respected man at home, and his English is excellent."

"So is yours," Lisa said. "and you don't have much of an accent."

Mikhail wiped his chin. "I couldn't speak a word of English when I first arrived in America. But I learned from the teacher at the embassy school, and I watched television, especially the baseball games. And I tried to make my mouth talk like the American baseball announcers. It's not perfect, but I get better."

"It's terrific," Lisa insisted. "I doubt I'd be able to do as well in Russia. I'm a big baseball fan, too. I love the Cincinnati Reds. Do you root for the Reds?"

Mikhail frowned. "The Mets," he said firmly. "The Mets are the best."

"It would be neat to see a Reds-Mets game," Lisa said. She slid her hand under her chin and rested her elbow on her knee. "But I keep interrupting. I'll shut up. I promise. I want to hear about you."

"I, too, would enjoy that," Mikhail replied. "I have seen baseball only on television. I would very much like to go with you to such a game." He paused. He had finished the hamburger, and he poked the remaining potato salad with a fork. Suddenly, he wanted to talk about baseball instead of himself. But he couldn't stay in Lisa's garage without telling her why he was here. She had kept him hidden and had brought him supper. At the very least, he owed her an explanation.

"My father had been told he was to head the consulate in Cincinnati, and I was very excited. But something happened in Moscow. I don't know what it was, but we were told that we would have to go back. We are supposed to leave from New York in a week." He put the fork down and looked at Lisa. "I don't want to go. I like America. I like the people and the cars and the baseball games. I like the fact that people can do anything they want without the Party's approval. At home, you cannot advance if you are not a Party member, and even so, the Party gives orders that make no sense."

Lisa wrinkled her nose. "I don't understand."

Mikhail sighed. He stood up and shoved his hands in his pockets. "Let me try to explain." He began to walk slowly around the table, as if the walk would help him find the words.

"My father's younger brother, my uncle, is a test pilot for the Russian Air Force. He is very, very smart. All his life he wanted to be a pilot. So did many others. But at home, to be a pilot you must first be selected to go to a special school. You are tested, and tested again. My Uncle Andrey passed. Many people did not. When he graduated, he needed more courses from the University. But again there were tests, and again, most people did not get in. Uncle Andrey did. Then he had to apply for special pilot's school. More tests. More failures. But Uncle Andrey made it. He studied very hard. Perhaps too hard, for his grades were so good, the air force decided he should be an instructor, not a test pilot. Uncle Andrey was very unhappy. He said he wanted to fly a plane, not a desk. But he did what he was told and taught

20

people to fly for several years. He kept attending all the Party meetings and kept talking to all the officials, and finally, someone signed a form and Uncle Andrey got to be a test pilot. He is brilliant. He is one of perhaps two hundred test pilots in the whole country. There are hundreds of millions of people in the Soviet Union, and of them, millions who want to do what he does, but Uncle Andrey is one of the privileged few. He gets special housing, special food, special uniforms."

"He sounds very smart," Lisa said.

"He is. And the country appreciates him. Even so, when the wheat needed to be harvested on the Ukraine, all the pilots were sent into the countryside with soldiers, teachers, doctors, actors, carpenters, construction workers, everybody—and told to harvest the wheat."

"I don't understand," Lisa said. "Why didn't the farmers do it? What do all those other people know about harvesting wheat?"

Mikhail slammed his hand on the table. "Exactly. They don't know anything about farming, so it *is* silly and inefficient to have them do the harvest, but that is how the government works in Russia. Even if you are one of the most special people in the country, you have to do whatever the government tells you." He paused, then said, "but I hear things have changed at home since Gorbachev came to power. He is trying to get rid of the stupid things and allow people more freedom to speak out. *Glasnost,* it is called, openness. But he is just one man, and there are so many others, so many who have always done things their way and won't change, won't want to change. Such a waste of talent and time." He shook his head slowly. "It isn't right. It isn't done that way in America."

"And you want to stay in America because you don't want to harvest wheat?"

He looked down at her. "No, *malenkaya devotchka.* It is not the wheat, it is the principle." He sat down. "I have spent half my life in this country. My American half wants your American freedom. In the Soviet Union, freedom is not worrying about finding a job, because the government finds one for you; it is not worrying about finding a place to live, because the government finds one for you. Here in America, the decisions are yours. I like that."

Lisa was silent for a moment. Then she said suddenly, "What was that you called me?"

"*Malenkaya devotchka?* It means 'my little girl'."

Lisa sat up straighter. "I am *not* a little girl! I'm eleven years old. You don't look much older."

Mikhail admitted, "I am twelve. It was not an insult, what I called you. It is a nice thing, a . . . how do you say . . . endearment."

"Oh." Lisa blushed. "I thought it was something like 'shorty' or 'small stuff.' That's what my brother calls me. He's almost sixteen and thinks he knows everything."

Mikhail sat down on the cot. The springs creaked. "Is Scott your only brother?"

Lisa nodded. "But my Mom is going to have a baby in October." She grabbed his wadded-up paper napkin and threw it at the crib in the corner. "Then we're going to need that stuff, and I'll probably have to share my room."

"Don't you want a new baby?"

"Absolutely not!" She jumped up so abruptly her chair fell over backwards. "My Mom's too old! She shouldn't be having a baby at her age. She's really happy and excited, but it's just ridiculous!"

"It sounds like you're jealous."

"Thank you, Dr. Belkin!" She stalked toward the stairs.

"Lisa, wait! I'm sorry." Mikhail held out his hand. "I don't mean to upset you. You have been so kind to me."

Lisa stopped and turned to face him. "I'm sorry, too," she said in a lower voice. "I didn't mean to yell."

Just then a car pulled into the garage below them.

Lisa rushed over to the table and grabbed the plate and fork. "That's Ben," she said quickly. "I've got to go. Stay up here tonight. Use the blanket from the car. I'll try to bring you a space heater for tomorrow night, along with more food and something to drink. We'll figure out what to do with you then."

The car door slammed.

"For goodness sake, be quiet!" she hissed back over her shoulder as she ran for the stairs.

At the bottom of the stairs a deep voice called up, "Anybody there?"

Mikhail hastily ducked behind the boxes. Lisa clattered down as fast as she could.

"Just me," she cried as she climbed down. "I decided to have supper in the old club house. You know, Ben, I might fix it up again."

Mikhail heard the stairs go back in place, then the man said, "You didn't forget to turn the light off, did you?"

Mikhail hopped up and flicked it off.

"I don't think so," Lisa said as they walked into the house together.

The room was pitch dark. The sun had set while he and Lisa were talking. When he could no longer hear voices, Mikhail crept along the wooden floor, searching for the flashlight. It was near the table where Lisa had dropped it. Mikhail flicked it on and tiptoed to the folded stairs. The blanket was beside them. He pulled it over to the bed and snapped off the light. He may as well try to sleep. He was tired and confused. Everything could wait till morning.

An hour later, Mikhail realized everything couldn't wait. He had to go to the bathroom. There was no bathroom in his attic. He snapped on the flashlight and looked at his watch. It was nearly ten o'clock. Was Lisa's family asleep?

As quietly as he could, Mikhail released the stairs so they dropped into the garage. They made a dreadful creak that seemed as loud as a thunderclap. Mikhail turned off the flashlight and sat as still as possible by the top of the stairs. He hoped no one would come to investigate the sound. No one did. After a few minutes, he turned the flashlight on again and eased his way down the stairs. The garage was dark. The door to the driveway was shut. He noticed a small electronic box near the door that led into the house. He presumed it was the garage door opener. The door to the house was also closed. What if it was locked? He would be unable to get inside. At that thought, he realized he had to go to the bathroom very badly indeed.

Mikhail put his ear against the door and listened. He heard nothing. Gently, he tried the handle. It turned. He shoved the door open. He was thankful this door didn't creak. He was inside a short hall that led to the kitchen, and he could see that a light was on. And he heard the sound of a television set somewhere upstairs. He hoped the only people awake were watching TV and uninterested in coming to the kitchen for a late snack. There were two closed doors on either side of him. The first one he tried led to the basement. He shut it again. The next door was better. It was a lavatory. With a sigh of relief, he went in.

A few minutes later he was safe again in the garage attic. He pulled the blanket over his head, tried not to think of how worried his father must be, and fell asleep.

Chapter Four

Mikhail was awakened by the creak of the wooden stairs as they dropped into the garage. For one terrified instant, he could not remember where he was. Then it came to him. Feet thumped up the stairs. Mikhail rolled off the couch and scooted under it, still clutching the blanket. He pulled it over him and hoped he was hidden.

"Hey!" Lisa called sharply. "Where are you going?" Her voice was coming from the garage.

"Where do you think?" retorted Scott.

His voice sounded close. Mikhail tightened his grip on the blanket, as if it were some sort of magic shield that could protect him from discovery.

A second set of feet pounded up the stairs.

"What are you looking for? I'll get it for you." Lisa sounded anxious.

"My OSU sweatshirt," Scott replied. "I can't find it in my closet, so I figured it might be up in the trunk with the summer stuff."

"I'll look. Stay there. Go on back to breakfast. I'll bring it down."

"Lisa, what is wrong with you? You're acting

crazy. Is there something up here you don't want me to see?"

Lisa hesitated.

Suddenly Scott laughed. "My birthday present! You bought it already, and you're hiding it up here!"

Lisa's answering laugh sounded relieved. "Can't a girl have some secrets?" she asked.

Mikhail heard Scott walk back toward the stairs and start down. "All right," Scott conceded. "I'll let you hunt. I don't want to mess up any surprises."

Both Mikhail and Lisa said nothing until Scott returned to the house, then Lisa let out a big sigh.

"It's okay, Ivan, you can come out now."

Mikhail crawled out from under the couch and brushed off his clothes.

"That was close," Lisa said. "Are you all right?"

Mikhail nodded. "Does your brother come up here often?"

Lisa sat down on the couch. "Nobody comes up here much at all. Every spring Mom brings the winter clothes up for storage and takes the summer things down, and every fall it's the reverse. I can't believe that Scott chose today to hunt for his dumb sweatshirt!"

Mikhail dragged the blanket out and started to fold it. "Perhaps you had better look for his shirt. If you don't, he'll probably come back."

"You're right." Lisa walked over to the trunk, lifted the lid, and began to poke through the contents.

Mikhail studied her critically. Lisa wore a navy blue jumper and a soft pink blouse with lace at the collar and cuffs. She had on matching pink tights and black patent leather shoes. A navy blue ribbon held her blonde hair in place.

"You are dressed up," he observed.

"Huh?" Lisa turned, the sweatshirt in hand. "Found it," she said and waved the shirt.

"Your clothing," Mikhail gestured. "Why are you dressed up?"

"Oh." Lisa looked down and tugged at her skirt self-consciously. "Mom always makes me dress up for Sunday school."

"Sunday school? I thought American children just went to school Monday through Friday."

Lisa closed the lid of the trunk, then locked it. She sat on top of it and looked at him.

"Regular school goes Monday through Friday," she confirmed.

Mikhail frowned. "This is a special school then?" His brow cleared. "Oh, I see. This is a church school, yes?"

"Sort of," Lisa said. "Except I'm Jewish, so it's part of a synagogue. We learn Bible stories, Jewish history, stuff about the holidays, and I take Hebrew for an hour."

Mikhail's eyes widened. "You are a Jew? A Jew in Columbus, Ohio? I thought all Jews had to live in New York."

She made a face. "This isn't Russia, you know. People live wherever they want. Haven't you been in the country long enough to learn that? There are Jewish communities in many American cities. Mom grew up in Cleveland, but her family moved to California. Ben came from Chicago. My real father was from Louisville, Kentucky." She hopped down and started for the stairs. "Ivan, I'm going to be late. We can talk more later. Oh." She stopped and turned to face him. "I almost forgot. I'll leave for Sunday school in about an hour. Mom drives me and a couple other kids, then she stays at the temple to work in the Sisterhood gift shop till I'm done. Ben goes to play golf with some friends. He'll leave pretty soon and be gone all morning. Scott has a softball game. He's in a league and they play every Sunday. So no one will be home for a couple hours. We never lock the door from the garage into the house because the garage door locks electronically. That means you can get in if you want. I'll leave a box of doughnuts and a box of cereal on the kitchen counter. There's milk in the refrigerator, so help yourself to breakfast. Just clean up the dishes so no one will know you've been there. I'll be back up this afternoon, and we will figure out what to do about you then. Got to

30

go." She started down the stairs.

"Wait!" Mikhail called. When she paused and looked at him questioningly, he asked, "Doesn't Scott go to Sunday school with you?"

Lisa shook her head. "Nope. He had his bar mitzvah almost three years ago."

"What?"

Lisa grinned. "Stay out of sight. We'll talk later." She disappeared down the stairs, then sent them back up.

Bewildered, Mikhail watched a sunbeam shafting through the small window onto the dusty wooden floor. Already there was much about America that confused him.

Mikhail dusted his hands on his slacks, then he examined them. His hands were dirty, and his clothes were covered with dust and lint. The attic above the garage obviously had not been cleaned for a long time. And neither had he. Mikhail decided what he really wanted was a bath and some clean clothes. But the only clothes he had were the ones he was wearing. He had no idea how to go about washing his clothes at Lisa's house, or whether her parents even had a washing machine. He had just made up his mind he had to get used to the dirt when he noticed the trunk Lisa had sat on.

Mikhail went over and examined it. It was old and brown, with tarnished copper nailheads trimming the corners. He lifted the lid. Inside were all sorts of clothes, some obviously Lisa's and the rest Scott's. Perhaps Scott's clothes might fit. He picked up item after item, but everything was much too big. Scott must be almost full grown. Mikhail carefully folded the clothes and replaced them, then sat on the lid of the trunk to think.

Lisa's mother kept a folded crib in the corner. It looked well used, so it probably had been Lisa's. She had saved it a long time. If Lisa's mom saved a crib, perhaps she also had saved old clothes that Scott had outgrown.

The second trunk was full of adult clothing, but the third one was the jackpot. Almost at once Mikhail found a shirt, sweater, and pair of trousers that seemed just the right size. He couldn't find any underwear, so he guessed he would have to use his own. Now for a shower.

Mikhail let himself into the house and stood very still, listening. The only sound he heard was the ticking of a large, yellow kitchen clock. He had planned to take a bath at once, but he hesitated when he saw two boxes on the kitchen counter.

He washed his hands at the sink and opened the boxes. One contained Rice Krispies. He wasn't familiar with the product, but he assumed it was some sort of cereal. The contents of the second box were a total mystery. It contained wheel-shaped food that smelled sweet. Some sort of bread? He loved dark Russian rye bread, so he chose a brown one and experimentally bit into it. It was sweet . . . a cake. He turned the box around the read the front. He was much better at speaking English than reading it, but he tried to sound out the word.

"Duff-nut," he said aloud. That didn't sound right. What had his teacher told him about o-u-g-h sounds? "Dow-nut." It still seemed wrong. Then he remembered what Lisa said about breakfast on the counter. "*Dough*-nut," he said with satisfaction. The wheel-shaped cakes were doughnuts. Written English was such a peculiar language. Words with similar spelling were often pronounced differently—tough, bough, dough. English made no sense. Would he ever learn to read it well?

Mikhail made himself a bowl of cereal, finished the doughnut; then as Lisa had cautioned, he cleaned up the bowl and spoon he had used and put them away. Unless someone noticed the missing doughnut, chances were Mikhail would not be discovered.

After eating, Mikhail explored the house. It was a big house by Russian standards. Lisa's family had a living room, a dining room, a kitchen, three bedrooms, a large bathroom and a small bathroom. Perhaps they were rich. To have a home like that in Russia, they'd have to be very influential in the Communist Party, like his father. Even so,

Mikhail and his father didn't have a house. They lived in a two-bedroom apartment, a very nice one, but much smaller than this house. The house was almost as big as the consulate. If Lisa's family wasn't unusual, and other Americans had homes like this, what a rich country America must be! But his Russian teachers told him Americans were poor and only a few lived well. Those people were called capitalists, and they oppressed the workers. But on the drive from the consulate in Cincinnati to King's Island, Mikhail had seen many homes. Most of them seemed big, as big as this. Surely all the rich capitalists in America didn't live on that route!

Mikhail sat on the top step and tried to think it through. If Lisa's family was typical, then the teachers in Russia were wrong. But why would Russian teachers give students the wrong information? They taught that America was trying to catch up with Russia and envied Russia her good fortune. At the same time, during the harvests, for instance, Party leaders would say, "Work hard; be efficient. We must catch up with America." Were the Party leaders in Russia mistaken, or lying?

Mikhail shook his head. All that thinking confused him. He decided it was time to get cleaned up.

Mikhail found a clean towel in the bathroom

closet and turned on the water. The family had a shower. Good. He preferred showers to baths. He undressed, stepped in, and began to sing an old Russian folk song at the top of his voice. He'd never be a music star, but he loved to sing in the shower.

Still singing, Mikhail turned the water off and was drying himself when he heard something that made his heart stop. Someone was knocking on the door!

"Lisa? Is that you? Why didn't you go to Sunday school? Lisa?" It was Scott's voice.

Frantically, Mikhail looked for somewhere to hide. The only place available was the tub. He stepped in and pulled the shower curtain. He wrapped the towel around himself and felt water dripping down his legs. He mentally begged Scott to go away.

"Lisa, what's wrong? Lisa?"

Mikhail didn't move. He shut his eyes. He heard the door open slowly.

Chapter Five

"Hey! Whose clothes . . .? What's going on here?" Mikhail heard the curtain being ripped back and felt a draft. He opened his eyes.

A tall teen-aged boy stared at him from large dark eyes like Lisa's. Unlike Lisa, his hair was brown. Unlike Lisa, he was scowling.

"Who are you?" he asked, more puzzled than angry.

"Why aren't you at the baseball game?" was all Mikhail could think to say.

"What!"

Mikhail added hastily, "I'm sorry. I was dirty. I needed to take a shower. I didn't think anyone would be home. Lisa told me . . ."

"Lisa!" repeated Scott. "What does Lisa have to do with this?"

Mikhail shivered and pulled the towel closer. Scott noticed, shrugged and shook his head. In a kinder voice, he said, "Listen, you're freezing in there. Get dressed and we'll talk." He walked out of the bathroom and shut the door behind him.

While Mikhail buttoned the shirt and pulled the sweater over his head, he noticed the bathroom window. Perhaps he could crawl out of it, make his way across the roof, and hide until someone came home and opened the garage door. Then he could sneak back into the attic above the garage.

He opened the window and looked. The only way out was straight down, two stories. Mikhail sighed. He may as well face Scott. It was either that or break a leg jumping.

"Are you clean now?" Scott asked.

Mikhail nodded forlornly. Scott would call the police, and they would send him back to the consulate. He would be shipped home in disgrace.

"Don't look so scared. I won't hurt you. I make it a practice never to hurt strangers I find showering in my bathroom."

"I'm not scared," Mikhail said in a small voice. He risked a glance at Scott. Scott was smiling. When Mikhail realized that Scott was teasing him, he felt better almost at once.

"Come into my room," Scott said. "Let's talk."

Mikhail liked Scott's room. It had sturdy oak bunkbeds with bright red spreads, a desk cluttered with books, a chair with pajamas thrown carelessly on it, a fish tank, and major league baseball pennants tacked on the walls. A handful of change, a baseball cap, two yo-yos, and a framed picture were on the chest of drawers. Scott swept the pajamas onto the floor and motioned to the chair.

"Have a seat," he invited. He sat down on the bottom bunk. "Why don't we start at the beginning. I'm Scott Alexander. What's your name?"

Mikhail hesitated, then said, "John Peter Belkin."

"How do you do?" Gravely, Scott held out his hand and shook Mikhail's. "Now, suppose you tell me what is going on. Are you a friend of Lisa's?"

"Yes."

Scott spread his hands and grinned. "And?" he asked.

"And what?" Mikhail asked nervously.

"And why were you taking a shower in our house? Who let you in? I just got home, and the doors were locked."

Mikhail sighed. Scott would find out eventually. "I came in through the garage," he said.

"But the garage doors lock electronically when the cars are gone. How could you get in?"

"Through the attic."

"What attic? The one in the garage? Were you *hiding* there?"

Mikhail nodded.

"Since when?"

"Yesterday."

"Wow." Scott leaned back and thought. "Are you running away from home?" At Mikhail's nod, he added, "And Lisa's helping you. Huh." He got up and went over to the fish tank. He sprinkled a little food in and watched the multi-colored shapes dart upward to gobble the flakes that sifted through the water toward them. "Do you like tropical fish?"

"I have never seen them before," Mikhail confessed.

Scott turned to stare at him. "You're kidding!"

Mikhail flushed. "I mean, not in person."

"Come here. I'll show them to you."

"They are so full of colors," Mikhail said. "That blue one is so bright."

"Yup, she's a beauty, isn't she? Where are you from, John? You sound as far from home as these fish."

"My accent is bad," Mikhail mumbled and looked down.

"It's not your accent. You hardly have an accent. It's the way you phrase things."

Mikhail sighed. "I am running away from Russia," he said.

"Wow," Scott said again in a softer voice.

"I like America," Mikhail said. "I want to stay here. I like that most people have cars. Some families, like yours, have two. In Russia most people don't know how to drive, let alone have a car. I like the animals . . . the fish and cats and dogs. We don't have many pets in Moscow. I like the baseball. We don't have that, either. But most of all, I like the freedom to choose where you live and what you do and who you talk to." He sat down in the chair.

"When I lived in Washington, my father pointed out to me all the demonstrations in front of the White House. It seems every day there are people demonstrating about something, and it is a *different* something all the time. Sometimes it is military spending. Sometimes it is human rights. Sometimes it is the environment. And some of the demonstrators get very mean. They say all sorts of bad things about the president and senators and anyone else who doesn't share their opinions. My father says all the demonstrations prove that people in this country are very unhappy and oppressed. But you know what I think? I think it is just the opposite. I think they are free to say whatever they wish, even if it is an insult about a government leader. In my country, you never see demonstrations. When I ask my father why, he says because people in Russia are happy and respect their leaders. But I think it is just the opposite. Sure, many people love and revere the premier, but I can remember a time when I was very small and had a friend named Josef." He sat silently a moment and studied his shoes.

"What happened to Josef?" asked Scott. His mouth had dropped open during Mikhail's outburst, and he looked fascinated.

"Josef lived in the same building as I did."

Mikhail looked up again. "We were only little boys, five years old. We played together sometimes. One night after I was in bed I heard my mother and father arguing about something. I heard the name of Josef's father. I didn't know what he did. But he did something. The next morning the KGB came in a long black car. Two men in overcoats got out and went to knock on Josef's door. They shouted and knocked so loud that I could hear them in my apartment, two floors up. I wanted to go out and watch, but my mother wouldn't let me. She sent me to my room. So I looked out the window. The KGB were taking Josef's father away. They shoved him in a car and the car drove off, very fast. Later that day, Josef, his mother, and his sister moved away.

"Father said they were enemies of the people, and they were being sent far away to live in Siberia. It was because of something Josef's father had said or written. I didn't know which. Josef was just a little boy, like me. How could he be an enemy of the people? My father told me not to speak of it ever again, and never to mention Josef's name. I don't know what happened to his father. One of the other children whispered he had been sent to Vladimir, a very famous prison. Most people sent there never come back.

"When I told my mother what the child had said and asked if Josef's father had done some-

41

thing terribly wicked, she hugged me tight. She whispered that sometimes people were sent to prison for no good reason at all, that she had an aunt who had been sent to the same prison before I was born, simply because she had fallen in love with an American officer in Moscow during the Second World War. She told me I must never, ever repeat it, or the police might do the same to us." Mikhail shivered. "I never have told anyone till now," he added.

Scott sat in silence for another moment. Then he said, "That's incredible."

Mikhail gave him a lopsided grin. "If Josef's family had been American, his father might have been sent to Congress instead of prison." He sighed.

Scott scratched his head. "What do you want to do, defect?"

Mikhail made a rude noise. "Defect? Defect is for spies. I am not a spy. I am twelve years old. I just want to live in this country."

"Do you have any family or friends here?"

"Just Lisa." He hesitated, then said questioningly, "and you?"

Scott grinned and gave a brief nod. "And me," he confirmed. He looked at his wrist watch. "Perhaps we'd better get you back to the attic. Mom and Lisa are due back from the Temple in a few minutes."

Chapter Six

An hour later, Lisa appeared in the attic with a sandwich on a paper plate.

"Hope you like corned beef on rye," she said. "It's the last *chometz* for eight days. We will be celebrating Passover."

"What?" Mikhail asked, puzzled.

"*Chometz* is food that isn't kosher for Passover," Lisa answered as she put the plate and a big, juicy pear on the table.

"I don't understand those words," Mikhail said.

"Oops, sorry," Lisa said. "Passover is a Jewish holiday, the Feast of Freedom. It commemorates the time the Jews were led by Moses out of the land of Egypt, and God sent the ten plagues to force the Pharaoh to let them go. The Pharaoh—that was the king of Egypt back thousands of years ago—kept telling Moses no, he wouldn't release the Jews, who were his slaves. But after God sent ten plagues—everything from a swarm of locusts that ate all the crops to killing the first-born children of the Egyptians—the Pharaoh agreed. But the Jewish people had to leave in such a hurry, they didn't have time to let their bread rise before baking, so they baked it anyway. It came out flat as a sheet of paper. It's called *matzoh*. Jews eat it for eight days every year, beginning with the first night of Passover, to remember the time they were slaves. Regular bread is *chometz*. It can't be eaten during Passover, nor can any food with leavening or flour.

"We pack up all the dishes and put them up here till Passover is finished, and we use special dishes instead. Even now Mom is busy packing in the kitchen, so lunch is on paper plates. She was too busy to notice that I made an extra sandwich."

Mikhail suddenly said, alarmed, "Then your mother will be coming up here to store the dishes!"

Lisa tugged on a pigtail. "Relax," she said. "Scott and I will take care of the dishes." She studied him out of the corner of her eye. "Pretty tricky how you got Scott involved in helping to hide you."

Mikhail flushed. "I was a mess. I needed a shower. But Scott came home early and caught me."

"Lucky for you it wasn't Ben," Lisa said dryly. She tugged a box toward her and opened the lid. "Cups and saucers," she announced.

"Who is Ben?"

"My mother's husband. My real father died in a car accident when I was eight. Mom married Ben when I was ten."

"Do you like him?"

"He's okay. Not like my real dad. But he's pretty nice. Ben's just a stickler for rules. He's never had kids, you see, and doesn't know how to deal with me and Scott. He makes up all kinds of dumb rules, like no candy except on Sunday, and our rooms must be cleaned before we can get our allowance. If he finds you, he'll probably call the police because it's the proper thing to do."

"I'd better go, right now!" Mikhail said, and started for the stairs.

"Hang on!" Lisa grabbed his arm. "Scott and I will hide you."

"But you can't hide me indefinitely."

Lisa bit her lip. "I know," she said in a low voice. Then she brightened. "My granddad is coming for Sedar. He'll figure out what to do."

"Sedar?"

"The first night of Passover. It's a special ceremonial meal. It's my favorite holiday of the year. Now eat lunch. There are a bunch of *National Geographic* magazines in that corner if you want something to look at. They have lots of neat pictures."

Later that afternoon, Scott and Lisa came upstairs with the last load of dishes to be stored in the attic during the holiday.

"Scott has this absolutely stupendous idea," Lisa announced.

Mikhail dropped the magazine he had been examining. "What?"

Scott said, "We'll have Lisa ask Mom if you can come for Sedar."

Mikhail jumped up, alarmed. "But Ben would then call the police! That's what Lisa said two hours ago!"

"Relax," Scott told him. "Lisa will tell Mom you are a friend who has never seen a Sedar before, so she wants to have you join us."

"Sedar is neat," Lisa said. "And besides, the food is always wonderful. That way you'd get a really good dinner."

"Ben won't think of you as a Russian running away from Moscow. He would have no reason to. He'd accept you as my sister's friend. And, John Peter, that way you could meet Granddad."

Lisa turned to her brother. "John Peter? What are you talking about? His name is Ivan Petrovich."

Mikhail shifted uncomfortably. "I have to talk to you about my name," he began.

Scott interrupted. "Lisa, John Peter is the English version of Ivan Petrovich. You can't call him Ivan at dinner, or Ben might catch on for sure."

"Okay," Lisa said. "John Peter sounds good to me." She headed for the stairs. "I'll go ask Mom."

"Wait!" Mikhail called, but she was already disappearing down the stairs.

"Come here," Scott said as he walked over to a thick garment bag hanging on a rack in one corner. "Somewhere in this bag is an old jacket of mine. It's plain navy blue and will go with just about anything including those old gray trousers of mine that you're wearing." His eyes twinkled.

"You see, I didn't have any clean clothes to change into," Mikhail started to explain.

"Forget it," Scott said. "They don't fit me anymore. You're welcome to them. Let's see what else we can find."

They came up with a white shirt and a blue and red striped tie, and even a pair of black shoes. They were a little tight, but Mikhail was so grateful to Scott, he didn't object.

He was dressed when Lisa came for him about five-thirty. She had changed out of her blue jeans and tee shirt into a light blue dress trimmed with yellow and white ribbons. She had combed out her pigtails and had tied a white and yellow ribbon in her hair.

"Why, Ivan, you look so handsome!" she exclaimed.

Mikhail could feel himself blush. No girl had ever called him handsome before. "Thank you," he said awkwardly. "You are very pretty, too. That is a lovely dress."

Lisa looked down, smoothed the skirt, and

smiled. "Thank you," she said. "It's new. Mom always gets me a new dress for Passover. Let's go. Everybody is here already."

When they entered the kitchen, Lisa's mother had her back to them. She was fussing over a dish on the counter.

"Mom, this is my friend, John Peter Belkin. John Peter, this is my mother, Ruth Meyer."

She turned around, and Mikhail found himself facing a taller, more elegant version of Lisa. Her blonde hair was cut short and her brown eyes had traces of mascara on the lashes. Her tan dress hung loosely from the shoulders, and her pregnancy was just beginning to show. Her broad smile reached her eyes. Mikhail found himself liking her very much.

"John Peter, we are so glad to have you join us tonight. Lisa says you are new to the city and that your father is out of town. I'm pleased you are here, so you won't have to be alone tonight."

"It is very kind of you to have me," Mikhail replied.

Mrs. Meyer turned to her daughter. "Really, Lisa, you should have brought him through the front door, not the garage. What will he think!"

Hastily, Lisa tugged on his arm. "Come on into the living room, John Peter. You can meet the rest of the family."

All of a sudden, Mikhail longed to go back to

the safety of the attic. He didn't want to face a room full of strangers, Americans who would probably figure out, in about thirty seconds, that he was a Russian. Despite the fact that Mikhail had spent half his life in the United Stated, he really had had very little contact with Americans except a few government officials, and they had just rumbled polite greetings to him before his father sent him on his way. Living in the embassy meant you lived with Russians, you ate with Russians, you went to school with Russians. Until his flight from King's Island, Mikhail's only real contact with Americans had been by television. As he trailed Lisa into the living room, a half dozen faces turned to smile at him. Just seeing that many smiles made him feel a bit more confident.

"Everybody, I want you to meet my friend, John Peter Belkin. John Peter has never been to a Sedar before, so I wanted him to join us."

"How do you do?" he mumbled.

"Lisa, that introduction won't do at all. John Peter is bound to feel overwhelmed by all this family," said a large, hearty man with a thick thatch of white hair and a matching mustache. He grabbed Mikhail's hand and gave it a firm squeeze, then put his arm around the boy. "You must tell him everyone's name so he can have a fighting chance. But son," he leaned over and his blue eyes beamed at Mikhail, "don't be embarrassed if you forget everyone's name as soon as you hear it. I always did on the first day of class. It took me at least a week before I was able to recognize my students' faces, let alone hook up the right names to them."

"Why, you look just like Father Frost!" Mikhail blurted out, then immediately wished he hadn't.

"Who?" asked a girl about Scott's age. "He looks like *who?*"

Something flickered behind the old man's eyes, but the smile stayed in place.

"Father Frost is his priest," Scott improvised hastily. "He thinks Granddad looks like his priest."

The old man serenely ignored them. "Now I," he told Mikhail, "am Professor Daniel Alexander, and the professor part is strictly emeritus, which means I am retired. I get to use the library and faculty facilities at Ohio University all I like, but I don't have to attend all those dreadful department meetings. I can stay on my farm in southern Ohio and edit English textbooks to my heart's content. It's a lovely, peaceful place, my farm. Perhaps Lisa will bring you down with her one day soon."

He guided Mikhail over to the couch. "This young lady, the one who asked the impertinent question, is also my granddaughter, Amy Kahn. That's her sister, Kathy, munching on those pecans. They're mighty tasty. Have some, John

Peter, I toasted them myself."

Mikhail slipped one into his mouth. They were good. He chewed and began to relax as Lisa's grandfather guided him around the room.

"You know Scott, I see, but do you know Ben Meyer? No? He's Scott and Lisa's stepfather, and a mighty fine fellow. And here are my daughter and her husband, Amy and Kathy's parents. Margie and Jack, I want to present John Peter Belkin. John Peter, Dr. and Mrs. Kahn."

In keeping with the strangely formal introduction, Mikhail made a small bow.

Margie Kahn clapped her hands in delight. "What beautiful manners!" she exclaimed. "How very European!"

Mikhail had a hunch he wasn't going to make it though the dinner without someone realizing he was Russian. So far, everything he said or did seemed to point out his differentness. Then he felt Professor Alexander pat him on the shoulder as if to reassure him.

"Not at all, my dear," the professor rumbled. "Just well brought up."

"Ding-a-ling," called Mrs. Meyer. "Dinner's almost ready, so let's start the Sedar."

When they walked into the dining room, Mikhail gasped. The table looked ready to serve royalty. It gleamed with silver dishes and crystal glasses. A deep red wine shimmered under the lights in a cut crystal decanter. An embroidered cloth covered what looked like a stack of large, flat crackers. Another plate bore a hardboiled egg, a bit of horseradish, more crackers, parsley and a small shank bone. One bowl held eggs, another held salt water. A third held a pink mixture Mikhail couldn't identify.

"It's beautiful," he breathed.

Mrs. Meyer smiled. "Thank you, John Peter. Why don't you sit next to Granddad, beside Lisa."

From his seat at the head of the table, the professor passed out half-moon shaped pieces of satin to all the males. Mikhail had no idea what it was, so he watched to see what Scott did. Scott opened it and slipped it on his head. Mikhail opened his and looked at it. It looked like a beanie.

Scott noticed him studying the hat and explained, "It's a *yarmulka*, a skullcap."

Mikhail nodded, and put it on.

Then the professor passed out thin books to each person. "These are *Haggadas*," he told Mikhail. "They are special prayer books for Sedar that contain the story of Passover. We all take turns reading the story out loud." Mikhail opened his book and noticed with dismay that while it had English on one page, it had a strange language on the other. He had never seen script like it before.

Lisa said as if to reassure him, "We only read a couple things in Hebrew, the various blessings, for instance. The rest is in English."

That didn't reassure him at all. So the strange language was Hebrew, and he wasn't expected to read it, but he *was* expected to read the English. And his English reading skills were terrible! His teacher was always yelling at him to practice more. But he had reasoned that if he could speak English fluently, why did he need to read it? Now he wished he had listened to his teacher. He sneaked a glance at Ben. Ben, no doubt, would realize from his poor reading skills that he was a Russian, and would call the police. Ben leafed through the book and ignored him.

Chapter Seven

The Sedar turned out to be the most fascinating meal Mikhail had ever attended. It was a ceremony with story, prayer, singing, and much laughter. Each of the items on the Sedar Plate had a special prayer and a special symbolism. They ate the parsley, dipped in salt water, before the meal began. They drank four glasses of wine. They put the horseradish, the bitter herb, between the *haroset*, the reddish mixture. The bitter herb recalled the bitterness of slavery, while the *haroset*—a mixture of chopped apples, nuts, cinnamon and wine—which Mikhail liked very much, symbolized the mortar that the Jews used to make bricks for the Egyptians. Lisa chanted the Four Questions in Hebrew and English. They capsulized the story of Passover. The family recited the ten plagues, and the Professor held aloft the shank bone of a lamb, to remind them of the most terrible plague of all, the one that finally forced the Pharaoh to let the Jews go: in each house that did not have the blood of a lamb on its door, the eldest Egyptian child was killed. They then ate the unleavened bread, *matzoh*, to remind them of the haste of the Israelites' flight from Egypt.

Finally, the Professor raised the plate of *mat-zoh* and said solemnly, "This is the bread of affliction that our fathers ate in the land of Egypt. Let all who are hungry come and eat. Let all who are in need come and celebrate the Passover with us. Next year in Jerusalem, may the entire house of Israel be free." Then he looked around the table at the faces of his dear ones and improvised another prayer. He said, "Dear Lord, soften the hearts of the Soviet leaders toward our brothers and sisters in the Soviet Union, so they may leave and come into freedom, so they may practice the Jewish religion without fear of reprisal."

Mikhail felt shivers run down his spine at the ancient words and the impromptu prayer. He remembered people making fun of Jews in Russia, but he never paid much attention to it. He had never before thought of what it must be like to be disliked by everyone because you are different. He had never thought of Jews as a people held captive. Jews were a different people in a society where the state disapproved of differences. He wondered what the Jews in his homeland were saying at their Passover services tonight, and then he realized that perhaps they weren't having any; they weren't allowed. The Soviet government frowned on the practice of religion. If you practiced your religion, you weren't hauled away to jail. Instead, you were denied privileges and promotions. Perhaps Jewish children couldn't go to the universities.

Mikhail never met any Jews in Moscow, but he knew members of the Russian Orthodox Church. Most were old people who went into the churches to pray. There were some young families that followed the old religion, but none his father associated with. In school his teachers taught the children that God was a fairy tale, and religion was designed to keep the workers downtrodden. Karl Marx had called it "The opiate of the masses."

Family members took turns reading the story of Passover. "In every age and every generation men have risen up and sought to destroy us," read Ben. "But the Holy One, blessed be He, always delivered us from the hands of oppressors." Ben's large eyes, magnified by his glasses, blinked owlishly. He ran a hand through his thinning hair.

Mikhail knew that six million Jews had been killed by the Nazis during World War Two. Surely the Nazis were dreadful oppressors. Two of his uncles had died fighting for the Soviet Union, fighting against the Nazis. Were his uncles some of those deliverers?

Scott read, "In each and every generation it is a person's duty to regard himself as though he went forth out of Egypt, 'And thou shalt tell thy son in that day, saying, this is done because of that which the Lord did for me when I came forth from Egypt.' Not our fathers alone did the Holy One redeem, but us, too."

Mikhail looked around the table at the shining, serious faces and decided Marx was wrong. God was not a fairy tale and religion was not a drug. God was real to these Jews, and religion was a moral force in their lives. It taught them respect for each person's human dignity. It taught them to value and celebrate freedom. And freedom was worth celebrating, Mikhail decided, freedom to say, think, and be what you want. Mikhail suddenly was very glad he was here.

But everything wasn't solemn. There were songs and jokes and a wonderful meal. Everyone seemed to like each other. Even when Scott teased Amy about her new boyfriend, and she called Scott a creep, there was a steady undercurrent of affection. Mikhail wished he belonged to such a family. For the last six years it had been just he and his father, and much of the time Mikhail had been left alone. His father was a busy man, with many important duties. For the first time in many years, Mikhail missed his mother terribly.

"Ben will drive you home," Ruth Meyer said later that evening.

Mikhail shot a look at Lisa. Her eyes were large, startled. Neither of them had thought of that possibility.

"It's okay," Mikhail said. "I don't need a ride."

"Nonsense, it's getting dark out. what would your father think of us if we let you walk home alone?"

"His father's out of town," Lisa said hastily.

"All the more reason Ben will drive you."

Ben Meyer stood up. "I'll get my jacket."

"Hey," Scott said abruptly. "Forget it, Ben. It's nice of you, but I'll walk John Peter home. I know where he's staying, and I want to get some air, anyway."

Ben sat down, and Lisa let out an audible sigh of relief.

Mikhail thanked everyone and followed Scott out the door. Once they were at the sidewalk, Scott said in a low voice, "Whew! That was a close one!"

"I don't mind telling you I started to sweat when your mom asked your stepfather to get the car," Mikhail muttered. Suddenly, he stopped and raised his head, "Where are we going?"

"Keep walking, in case anyone is looking out the window," Scott said. Mikhail fell in step with him.

"We'll go around the block, then cut through the alley to the back of the house. You can hide in the bushes till I make sure the coast is clear. Then we'll sneak you back into the attic."

"Actually, it feels good to walk and stretch my legs. I have been cooped up inside too long," Mikhail said.

"Lisa told me you sneaked into the back of our car at King's Island, but how did you get to King's Island? It's a long way from the Soviet embassy in Washington."

Mikhail laughed. "It certainly is," he agreed. "And it's even longer to Moscow."

"What?"

"The Soviet government had decided to open a consulate in Cincinnati, and my father was supposed to be promoted to consul, which meant we would move to Cincinnati. I was excited because it meant for the first time I would live in America, away from the embassy. A consulate is much smaller than an embassy, fewer people, so I hoped I might even be sent to an American school. I would get to meet real Americans and see how they lived. I was very excited. But then something happened. I don't know what exactly. But someone else got the promotion instead of my father."

"Politics," Scott nodded. "It's everywhere."

"Yes. Well, my father told me we were being sent home after the ceremonies opening the consulate. The officials wanted me out of the way while they were getting ready for the opening. Someone suggested I might enjoy an American amusement park. I did." He grinned briefly. "I ran away."

They walked in silence for a moment. Mikhail watched their shadows lengthen and recede as the two boys crossed into a pool of light from a lamppost, then walked past it. Mikhail glanced up. It was a clear night, and he could see many stars.

"Funny," he murmured. "The stars look the same from Russia."

"My great grandfather came from Russia," Scott said.

"He did?" Mikhail stopped, astonished.

Scott stopped with him. "My father's grandfather. Professor Alexander's father. He came to this country in 1903."

"Why?"

Scott started to walk again. Mikhail kept up with him.

"Conditions were terrible in Russia then, but you know that," Scott said. Mikhail nodded. "The nobility made up only five percent of the population, but they seemed to have ninety-five percent of the wealth. The peasants, who had nothing, trusted the czar, but the czar really didn't know his people at all."

"The masses were oppressed by the capitalists," Mikhail responded. "I know our history."

"Well, not the capitalists, exactly," Scott said. "The capitalists were the merchants, and there was almost no merchant or middle class. It was just nobility and serfs. And a very weak king. Excuse me, czar. His wife was very strong-willed. They had a sick son."

"Who seemed to be helped by the mad monk Rasputin," added Mikhail. "I know all that."

"Sorry," Scott said. "I just like to tell things in order."

"Go ahead."

Scott shoved his hands in the pockets of his jacket. "Well, the court was minding the queen who was minding the monk, and no one was minding the country. The peasants were being taxed to death. They were miserable. Granddad told me that when people are miserable, they often look for someone else to blame or abuse, so they abused the Jews. They killed them in mass riots called pogroms. That sort of thing had been going on sporadically for centuries. But then some wiseguy hit upon an idea to stop Jews from being born at all. He decided if you drafted Jewish men into the army for twenty-five years, and *if* they came out alive, they'd be too old to father children, so the Jews would die off."

"Wow," Mikhail muttered. Lisa's favorite expression seemed to fit.

"Well, Granddad's father didn't want to be drafted, so he hid out when his draft notice came. But pretty soon the soldiers started searching for him. His nephew was a lookout, and when he

61

spotted the soldiers riding up the dirt track that led to their village, he would come running up to the house to tell great-grandpa to hide. Great-grandpa would run out the back door just as the soldiers were trotting up. A stream ran behind the house. The soldiers posted lookouts along the water to grab him if he passed by. But great-grandpa hid in a hollow log and floated past them to safety. Eventually, he made his way to America, and when he came here, he hitch-hiked his way on wagons and carts to Kentucky, where he had a distant relative. He slept in haystacks and did farmers' chores for food. He did all that without knowing English. And he was only sixteen." Scott paused and shook his head. "I'm going to be sixteen in two weeks. I can't imagine doing that."

Mikhail was silent. Scott stopped and motioned to some bushes.

"This is our backyard," Scott said. "I'll hide you here until I can sneak you back into the attic. Let me just run ahead and see if the coast is clear. If so, I'll wave to you and you can come on to the garage."

Chapter Eight

The next morning, Mikhail was awakened by the sound of a car's engine below him. He peeked out the window and watched Ben back out his car and drive away. A few minutes later, Lisa appeared with a paper bag and a thermos.

"There's plenty of food in the bag," Lisa told him. "Turkey and cheese and fruit and some of Mom's Passover brownies. They're made without flour, but they're yummier than the regular kind. There's milk in the thermos."

"Thanks," said Mikhail as she put the bag and thermos on the small table.

"I have to leave for school today," Lisa announced. "Spring break starts on Wednesday. You can't stay up here indefinitely."

"I know," Mikhail replied. "I've got to figure out what to do. It's terrific of you to hide me, but it can't go on forever."

Lisa nodded. "What do you think of this idea? Scott and I were talking last night, and we thought, if it's okay with you, we'd do this: you come to school with me tomorrow. We don't do much on the day before vacation, and I'll tell the teacher you're my cousin who came for a visit.

You can see what American school is like. Then Wednesday, Granddad is taking Scott and me back with him to his farm. We'll hide you in the back of the car, just like you hid in the back on the way up from King's Island. Granddad's awfully smart. And he can keep a secret. I'll bet he can figure out how to help you."

Mikhail nodded uncertainly. "I guess that's all right. He seems like a very nice man."

Lisa hesitated, then said, "Are you going to be okay by yourself all day? I know it's sort of boring, but I thought after school is out, perhaps you and I could go to Northland Mall to hunt for a birthday present for Scott. I'll tell Mom I want your expert opinion," she grinned. "I'm sure she'll take you, too."

"What is a mall?" asked Mikhail

Lisa was so surprised, she sat down on the couch. "A mall? You've never heard of a mall?"

Mikhail shook his head.

"It's a big shopping center under one roof. There are lots of stores. There are trees and benches and fountains inside, and it's really neat. Sometimes older kids hang out there."

"Sort of like the GUM department store in Moscow," he suggested, "a big government store where you can buy lots of things."

"Nope. It has nothing to do with the government. Different people own these stores, and what they make from selling, they keep. Of course, they have to pay taxes. Everyone has to pay taxes. But the more business they do, the more money they make."

"Capitalism," said Mikhail.

Lisa shrugged. "It's the American way. That's what Ben says. He owns a hardware store." She bit her lip and looked at him thoughtfully.

"Is something wrong with his store?" Mikhail asked.

"Huh? Oh, no." Abruptly, Lisa reached around to the paper bag, opened it, and drew out a newspaper. "It's something else." Hesitantly, she unfolded the paper and showed it to him.

Mikhail gasped. His own picture stared back at him from the front page. "Russian Boy Kidnapped" screamed the headline. He pulled the paper onto his lap and frowned at the letters, struggling to read them.

After a moment he handed the paper back and said ruefully, "My teacher always told me I'd regret the day I couldn't read English well. Can you help me with the words?"

Lisa began:

"The Russian embassy has filed a protest with the American government regarding the disappearance of the twelve-year old son of an embassy official. The boy was last sighted at the King's Island Amusement Park near Cincinnati.

Embassy spokesman V. Minkov says the boy was grabbed as he stepped off a ride by a dark-haired man in a trenchcoat. Minkov stated, 'The kidnapper showed an FBI badge while his partner pulled a gun out and dragged the boy away. The men guarding the boy were afraid the child would be shot, so they didn't follow at once. As a result, they soon lost the boy and his kidnappers in the crowd.' The FBI denies the story vigorously and labels it a fabrication."

"Ridiculous!" Mikhail exploded. "There weren't any FBI men! And Minkov himself was one of my guards. He and Kobatchnick are so fat, they couldn't keep up when I ran away. He's lying so he won't get into trouble with his superior."

Lisa gave a short laugh.

"Don't you believe me? You must believe me! I hid in your mother's car!"

"Calm down," Lisa said. "Of course I believe you. Russians always lie. Besides, it was so hot that any man in a trenchcoat would have melted into a little puddle."

"What do you mean 'Russians always lie,' " Mikhail demanded.

"Well, maybe not *always*," Lisa backed down, "but they lie so often it's like the boy who cried wolf. He loved to cry wolf just to get attention, so the villagers began to ignore him. Then one day the wolf really did come. The boy hollered, but the villagers didn't believe him, so the wolf ate him.

Anyway," Lisa pointed out, "you yourself said Minkov was lying to protect himself."

Mikhail shook his head. "This is very confusing," he said.

Lisa picked up the paper. "There's more, mostly about the FBI denying involvement, and the government promising to help locate you. Do you want me to go on?"

"That's enough." Mikhail stood up. "I've got to get out of here before you and your family get into trouble."

"Nonsense," Lisa said firmly. "You're safe here. Both Scott and I will protect you. No one is going to come into the attic looking for you—not the embassy, not the FBI, not anyone." She glanced at her wristwatch and headed toward the stairs. "If I don't hurry, I'll be late. I'll see you after school. And don't worry. Mom will be gone most of the day. This is her day to volunteer at Children's Hospital. So you don't have to worry about being quiet or anything."

"Wait," he said. "Perhaps I shouldn't go to the mall with you after school. My picture was in the paper."

"That picture is blurry. It makes your hair look darker than it is, and it makes you look younger. No one will recognize you. Just take it easy."

The day dragged by. Mikhail watched Mrs. Meyer leave, then cautiously entered the house a few times to use the bathroom or get a glass of water. He leafed through old magazines and explored the attic, and for part of the afternoon, he slept. He was very glad when Lisa came home. She arrived just fifteen minutes after her mother.

They were climbing down the attic stairs when Mrs. Meyer came into the garage. Mikhail froze. She had caught them! Surely she would realize he'd been hiding in the attic, and she would call the police!

"Oh, there you two are. Up using the old club-house, hmm? Are you ready to go to the mall?" She fished in her purse for keys.

Mikhail and Lisa exchanged glances. Lisa rolled her eyes and mouthed, "Whew!"

"Hop in the car, kids. Once we get to North-land, I'll turn you loose. I have a few things to get in Lazarus, so we'll find a place to meet in an hour, okay?"

Mikhail enjoyed the ride. It was the first he had really seen of the neighborhood. There were so many houses! Each house had a garage and a yard and often a toy or bicycle out front. He mar-veled at the wealth of the country.

Where he came from, most people lived in apartments given to them by the state. Cars were unusual. Bicycles were not children's toys but adult transportation. Some of these streets had homes that were quite large—mansions by his standards. He decided he would like to live in a house. He could make as much noise as he wanted and his father wouldn't tell him to be quiet for fear that he'd disturb the neighbors. If he lived in a house, he wouldn't hear the neighbors' fights, or their radios. He and his father could have all the privacy they wanted.

Perhaps, when they returned, the state would reward his father with a *dacha*, a house in the woods outside Moscow. He had visited some, but his father had not been important enough to rate a *dacha* before. If they lived in a *dacha*, he could get a dog!

Then Mikhail realized he and his father would not be together. His father was returning to Russia in less than a week. He'd have a *dacha* near Moscow and Mikhail would have one in Ohio. Living alone in Ohio didn't seem like much fun.

Chapter Nine

When they reached Morse Road, Mikhail forgot his somber thoughts. There were so many stores! Some sold flowers, some sold furniture, and that big one over there sold toys. All that room just for toys! The thought staggered him. If these were separate stores, then what a wonder a mall must be!

The mall took his breath away. It was huge! The parking lot alone was enormous. It seemed to cover acres of land, and it was full of cars.

"This is so big!" he said in wonder.

Mrs. Meyer glanced at him in the rearview mirror. "You think so? You must come from a smaller town. Northland is really pretty standard in size. Bigger cities have even bigger malls. Some malls in Cleveland, where I grew up, have two stories."

When they entered through a side door, he stopped in delight. Color was everywhere. Colored lights illuminated fountains and spelled out store names in every shade of the rainbow. Trees did grow in tubs inside the mall as Lisa had promised. The stores boasted big windows full of a blinding variety of merchandise.

"Okay, kids, it's 3:35. I'll meet you here in an

hour." Ruth Meyer smiled at them. "Have fun, and don't be late."

Lisa grinned at Mikhail's bewilderment. "There's a lot to take in, isn't there?" she said. "How about if we just walk and window-shop for a few minutes? I know, I'll buy you a giant chocolate chip cookie at the cookie shop. They're terrific. Then we can decide where we want to go."

They smelled the shop before they saw it. The rich, sweet aroma seemed to reach out and draw them in. Lisa bought two giant cookies and handed him one.

"This is very delicious," he told her after the first bite. "What do you call this delicacy?"

Lisa laughed. "A chocolate chip cookie. You mean cookies are new to you, too? Oh, wow."

"I have eaten cookies," he said defensively. "Russians like cookies. Have you ever had a Russian tea biscuit? They're excellent. But the chocolate chip is new to me."

Lisa smiled apologetically. "Sorry," she said. "I didn't mean to laugh. Come on. Let's walk."

They poked in a bookstore, a record shop, and clothing stores. Mikhail was dazzled by the gold and diamonds in a jewelry store.

"Surely these things are very expensive," he said. "Only for the rich."

"Well," Lisa said, "some of them are real expensive, and only for the rich. But most of the stuff is reasonably priced. Not for someone like me, on an allowance," she added hastily. "But some of the necklaces, well . . . look, see that one in the corner, the gold drop with a pearl and three little rubies? Ben got Mom one like it for their anniversary, but Ben isn't rich. He just saved some extra money for a couple months and bought it because he knew Mom would like it."

"Oh, I don't believe you," Mikhail scoffed.

"It's true," Lisa said. "Mom wore it for Sedar last night. Don't you remember?"

He thought back and did recall seeing the dainty necklace around Ruth Meyer's neck. "Are you sure Ben isn't rich?" he asked doubtfully.

Lisa smiled and tugged on his arm. "Come on. I want to look in the pet store."

When they reached the window, Mikhail caught his breath, then burst out, "Little dogs! They sell little dogs here!"

"Puppies," Lisa corrected. "Isn't that black and white one cute? Let's go in. I want to pet him."

They entered the door and reached into the pen that held four wriggling pups. She held out her hand to stroke the black and white puppy, but a tan dog leaped up and licked her before she could touch the first animal. She giggled, and used both hands to stroke the two of them at the same time. Then an all-white and an all-black dog spotted her and climbed on top of their litter mates to be pet-

72

ted. Hesitantly, Mikhail reached out his hand. The tan dog snuggled under Mikhail's fingers, then began to nip them happily.

"This brown puppy is wonderful," Mikhail exclaimed. "I like him the best."

"He's a pushy little fellow," Lisa said. "He wants all the attention first."

A tall young man in a white apron came over to them and grinned. "Those pups are mutts, so they're on special, kids. No pedigrees, just lots of fun. And just twenty-five dollars a dog."

Lisa stroked the all-black puppy longingly. "I have enough money in my bank account, but Mom won't let me get a dog right now. She's expecting a baby, and she says no puppy till the baby is at least a year old."

"How about a hamster then?" The man pointed to a sign that said, in red letters, "Hamster Special two dollars each."

Lisa straightened up and put her hands in her pockets. "No pets today. Mom wouldn't approve. Sorry." She turned to walk out the door.

"Keep working on her, kid. Maybe she'll let you have a rabbit for Easter," the man said.

"We're Jewish," Lisa replied.

"A fish for Passover, then."

Lisa laughed and waved at him. "I'll be back in about a year. I'll wait for the puppy."

The man laughed, too. "Come back any time.

Our puppies like to be petted."

As they walked back into the mall, Mikhail said, "I have always wanted a dog. But my father says the embassy is no place for a dog. And in Moscow very few people have them."

Lisa stared at him. "Hardly anyone has a dog in Moscow?"

"Not when I was little. Oh, maybe a movie star would have a very little dog. But I never saw one on the street, and certainly none of my friends had them. Things have changed recently, but it is still unusual to have a dog. My mother told me that one time she saw a small crowd near Red Square. When she went over to see what was happening, she saw a foreign lady walking a dog. People had gathered around to watch and perhaps touch the dog."

"Sounds like what would happen here with a circus animal."

"I saw more circuses than I saw dogs," Mikhail said.

"I've never been to the circus," Lisa confessed.

"No? Russia has wonderful circuses, the best performers in the whole world. My father took me to the circus at least twice a year in Moscow. The performers are such marvelous acrobats, and so brave. The costumes glitter and the sawdust smells wonderful. There are lots of mean lions and tigers and always a man with a whip who trains them. The elephants and horses have fancy saddles."

"The *elephants* have saddles?" Lisa interrupted.

"Certainly. And only the most beautiful of circus ladies are allowed to ride them."

"Now you're putting me on!"

"That means what?"

"You're teasing me," Lisa said.

"I am not," Mikhail insisted. "When you come to Moscow to visit, I will show you."

"Ivan, you're not going back to Moscow, remember?"

He stopped, thunderstruck. "Of course," he said quietly. "I forgot." He felt a cold, hard knot in the pit of his stomach. He would never see a Russian circus again.

"Ivan," Lisa said gently. "I didn't mean to make you sad."

"It's okay," he said.

"I'm sure there are as many things about Russia that would surprise me as there are things about America that surprise you," Lisa observed. "Let's go back to the record shop. There's a Bruce Springsteen album that Scott would like. Then I want to stop in the toy store and pick up a yo-yo."

"A yo-yo?" Mikhail asked.

"Scott collects them."

A short time later, the album in a bag under her arm, Lisa steered Mikhail into the toy store.

He marveled over the number and variety of toys.

"I did not know there were this many toys in America," he said softly to her, as he squeezed down a row containing doll dishes on one side and action figures on the other.

"This is just a small store," Lisa said. "Yo-yos are on that counter over there."

He picked up one of the circular toys curiously and turned it over. "Two pieces of wood attached to a string."

"The string is attached to the wood," Lisa corrected.

"What do you do with it?" Mikhail asked as he turned it over in his hand.

"Watch." Lisa hooked a loop in the string around the second finger of her hand, released the yo-yo with a snap, and stroked it up and down.

Mikhail laughed. "It climbs the string and slides down again. What a clever toy!" He watched in amusement for a moment, then asked, "May I try it?"

Lisa showed him how to fit the string over his finger and described what he should do. He released the yo-yo, and it tumbled to the end of the string and hung flat. He jerked his arm upward, but the yo-yo stubbornly clung to the bottom of the string and twisted in circles.

"It looked so easy," he said ruefully.

"It takes practice," Lisa told him. "I couldn't do

it cither the first couple of times I tried it. Scott is really good at it. He can do all kinds of tricks with yo-yos. I'll give him his yo-yo tonight, and he can show you how."

"Can I help you?" asked a middle-aged woman in a red smock. She looked at them suspiciously, like she thought they had no intention of buying anything.

"Two yo-yos please," Lisa said crisply. She handed the woman a red one and a yellow-and-blue striped one, along with two dollars from her purse.

The woman began to hand Lisa the change, then stared at Mikhail. "You know," she said slowly, "you look familiar."

"He shops here a lot," Lisa improvised and reached for her money. But the woman pulled it out of Lisa's reach without taking her eyes off Mikhail.

"No," she continued, "that's not it. Hey, Wally, come here a minute. Don't this kid look familiar?"

"I'll take my money," Lisa said.

Wally walked over and studied Mikhail. "You mean like he was in a TV commercial or something? In the papers, maybe?"

Lisa leaned across the counter and grabbed her change from the saleswoman's hand.

"That's it," the woman said in a loud voice. "He looks like that kidnapped Russian boy."

"Run!" Lisa hissed at Mikhail.

He didn't have to be told twice. He caught up with Lisa and together they pounded down the mall toward the big department store.

"Hey!" hollered the woman. "Wally, call the cops!"

As they reached a support post, Lisa grabbed his shirt. "Hold it," she wheezed.

He clawed at her fingers to free them from his shirt. "We must run!" he said desperately. "You heard that woman. She is calling the police."

"Listen to me," Lisa said. "If we keep running, people will stare. We must walk, blend in with the crowd. Otherwise they'll think we have a reason to run, and someone might stop us. It's time to meet Mom. We'll get in the car and go home and no one will bother us. Cool it, Ivan."

He drew in a deep breath, released it slowly. What Lisa said made sense.

"The cops will think she's nuts," Lisa added. "Do I look like a kidnapper in a trench coat? Do you look kidnapped?"

He laughed. "You're right," he admitted.

She released her grip on his shirt and reached in the small bag. She pulled out the yellow-and-blue yo-yo and handed it to him. "This is for you. A present."

Mikhail ran a finger over the gaily painted sides. "A present for me? You're giving me a present?"

She grinned at him. "Why not? You look like you could use a yo-yo."

"Lee-sa," called a woman through the crowd. "Lisa, hurry up."

Lisa smiled at him. "See? Mom's ready to take us home."

"Well, John Peter, where do I drop you off? What's your address?" asked Ruth Meyer as they swung out of the shopping mall parking lot onto a street heavily clogged with traffic.

Alarmed, Mikhail shot a look at Lisa. Lisa's brown eyes were enormous. Then she winked at Mikhail and put a finger to her lips.

"Mom, John Peter's dad is going to pick him up at the school. John Peter doesn't have a key to his house, so his father will have to let him in, and his dad's at work."

"Fine," said Mrs. Meyer. "We'll wait with you to make sure you're okay. Besides, I want to meet your father." She looked in the rearview mirror to smile at Mikhail in the back seat with Lisa. "He must be a special man to have such a nice son."

"He is very special," Mikhail said. "But, please, Mrs. Meyer, don't wait for my father. He might be late and um . . . um . . . you have to prepare dinner. I don't want to delay you."

"Nonsense, John Peter. I don't mind waiting." She stopped the car at a light.

Mikhail slumped back against the seat. Now he would be forced to tell Mrs. Meyer the whole story. She probably would tell her husband, and he would call the police. Would the police call the CIA? Would the CIA have him arrested as a spy? He had heard dreadful things about the CIA when he lived in the Russian embassy.

"Mom, for goodness sake! Don't hang around the school waiting for John Peter's father. You're treating him like a baby! If any of the other guys catch you waiting, they'll tease us both terribly. It's hard enough being the new kid at school without all the other kids hassling you!" Lisa burst out.

Mrs. Meyer was silent for a moment. Would it work? Would Lisa's tactic save him?

"All right," she said finally. "I won't wait. But I want you to promise if your dad is more than fifteen minutes late, you'll come right over to our house and wait there."

What a lovely girl Lisa was! She had done it!

"I promise," Mikhail said in relief. Then he added, "Thank you for being so understanding, Mrs. Meyer."

"John Peter, when I do get to meet your father, I plan to tell him what wonderful manners you have. I wish my two were as well-behaved."

"Mom," Lisa piped up indignantly, "what are you talking about? My manners are great . . .

when I'm not around you, I mean."

"Well, I'm glad *someone* gets the benefit of them," Mrs. Meyer said dryly.

Fifteen minutes after Mikhail was dropped off at the school yard, Lisa came to get him. She lived only a block away. He felt a lot safer in the attic.

Chapter Ten

The next morning, Mikhail was dressed and ready when Lisa came to get him. She held her books with one hand and put the other on her hip. She tilted her head and looked at him critically.

"Take off the jacket and tie. We're going to school, not to a Sedar service."

He looked down and touched the jacket. "It is too dressy, then?"

"Much too dressy. Look at me. I'm wearing a plaid shirt and a denim skirt." She dumped the books on the rumpled bed and went over to an open truck. She rummaged around for a moment, then came up with a short-sleeved, red-and-white checked shirt that belonged to Scott. "Take off that white shirt and put this on instead. Nobody wears long-sleeved white shirts to school unless they have to make a speech to the student body, for goodness sake."

He had begun to unbutton the shirt before she finished speaking. He took the other shirt from her and slid into it, buttoning rapidly. "I do not want to stand out." He added, "In my school, we wear uniforms."

"The kids will give you the once-over anyway because you are new, so you may as well look like you fit in."

"What will you tell them?"

"That you are my cousin from Washington, and that you're here for spring break. We'll just say you got out of school earlier than we did. They'll buy that. Are you ready? Good. No, you don't have to carry my books for me."

"Lisa, it is my honor," Mikhail said, and smiled at her.

She blushed and turned her head to hide it. "I'll go down first and make sure Mom doesn't come out. We better be quiet in the garage. She's in the kitchen and has ears like a bat."

"A bat?"

"You know. Extraordinary hearing. Bats use sonar or something to hear sound waves bouncing off the walls of caves so they don't fly into them."

"Where did you come up with that?"

Lisa shrugged. "I read a lot," she said.

Mikhail enjoyed the walk to school. It was only the second time he had been outside Lisa's house during the day. It had been several days since he had seen the sun. He marveled at how good the warm sun and soft spring breeze felt on his face. Trees were beginning to bud with small yellow-green leaves. Grass was sprouting through the old thatch of last summer. Bright yellow forsythia blossoms shone like stars on bushes. Tulips, hyacinths, and daffodils splashed more color in otherwise barren gardens.

"I love spring," said Mikhail.

"Me, too," replied Lisa.

The neighborhood consisted of middle-class homes, some two-story like Lisa's, some one-and-a-half. They were built of brick, frame, aluminum siding, and stone. Their shutters were painted brown or red or black or blue or green. Mikhail, used to the high-rise apartment buildings of Washington and Moscow, was amazed by it all.

"There is so much variety," he marveled. "Everyone has a different house."

"Well, everyone is a different person," Lisa said. She pointed to the right at the one-story brick school building shaded by many trees and surrounded on two sides by blacktop dotted with playground equipment. Children swarmed over the playground. Most seemed to be streaming for the double doors. "The bell must have rung. We'd better run. I don't want to be tardy."

Mikhail didn't know what being tardy meant, but he decided if Lisa didn't want it, he didn't either.

As they sprinted for the doors to join the line of children, three girls hollered, "Lisa!"

Lisa turned and smiled. "Hi, guys," she said.

One girl with long brown braids said shyly,

"Who's the guy carrying your books, Lisa?"

Mikhail smiled at her and her two companions.

"This is my friend, I mean, cousin, John Peter. He's visiting from out of town, so I brought him to school." She turned to Mikhail. "These are my friends—Emily, Beth, and Julie."

"How do you do?" he asked.

One of the girls giggled. "He's cute," she said.

Mikhail felt himself blush up to his hair roots. No girl had ever called him cute before. He wasn't sure if he liked it. Lisa took his arm and steered him past her friends.

"We've got to go," she called over shoulder. Then she said to Mikhail softly, "Don't let Julie get to you. She's just going through a phase. She's boy crazy."

"I don't understand," Mikhail whispered.

"Don't worry," Lisa reassured him. "Most guys don't either."

Lisa led him into a classroom. When he got to the door, he hung back. A half dozen faces turned curiously in his direction. He suddenly wasn't sure coming to school had been a good idea. Lisa turned back and tugged on his sleeve.

"Don't worry, they won't bite. Come on."

He followed her to the teacher's desk. A short, plump woman with frizzy red hair and kind brown eyes smiled at him.

"Mrs. Wilson, this is my cousin, John Peter

Belkin. He's visiting us for a couple of days from out of town, so I brought him to school with me."

"Welcome, John Peter. We're glad to have you. Why don't you take one of those chairs from the back of the room and pull it up to Lisa's desk? That way you can sit with her."

"Thank you," he said.

School was a surprise to him . . . it was easier than he expected. The math, especially, was surprisingly simple.

"You're kidding!" Lisa said in a disbelieving voice when he told her at recess. "I think it's awfully hard."

"We had this stuff three years ago," Mikhail said. "Your teachers don't push you. You are smart enough, but your teachers must think your brains are lazy. You don't learn languages. You don't study science, at least not any *real* science, just baby stuff about dinosaurs. School in America is very easy. Do you want a push?" He pointed to the swings.

"Sure," Lisa answered and got on. As Mikhail pulled her back toward him and prepared to release the swing, she asked, "Is there anything you *like* about my school?"

He hopped on the swing next to hers and thought. He pumped his feet until he and Lisa were swinging in tandem, then said, "I like how the students and teachers get along. Very informal, not threatening, except when the teacher yells at someone to be quiet, and even that isn't scary. It's obvious you like each other. It's easier to learn if you are not afraid. I also like that there are no political lectures." He leaned his head back and admired the clear blue of the sky.

"What do you mean?"

He sat up and pumped the swing again. "That's when a member of the Party comes into the classroom and tells us how much we should love Mother Russia and how hard we should work to be productive citizens."

Lisa laughed. "Propaganda." She wrinkled her nose. "No big cheese."

"What cheese?"

"No cheese. It's a figure of speech. It means no big deal. Your Party members are trying to brainwash you."

He hopped off the swing. "It's not brainwashing!"

Lisa dragged her feet, slowing the swing. "Ivan, don't get so upset. I thought you hated those lectures."

Mikhail sighed and looked down. "I do," he said in a dejected voice.

"Then what's wrong?"

He shook his head. "I don't know," he said. "If this were a vacation, I'd be having a wonderful time, but since I ran away, well . . ." His voice trailed off uncertainly. He looked at her with troubled blue eyes. "Everything is a lot more complicated than I thought it would be. I don't like not knowing what's going to happen to me."

Lisa nodded, her brown eyes solemn. "It can be pretty confusing. But tomorrow we'll go to Granddad's farm. He'll help us. He'll straighten things out, don't you worry."

The bell rang, ending recess. Children streaked from all corners of the playground to the doors, then pushed, shoved, and laughed their way inside. But once Mikhail was seated in Lisa's classroom, the teacher made an announcement that made him want to jump up and run outside again.

"I have a surprise," said Mrs. Wilson with a smile. "After lunch we'll have an assembly to hear a speaker from the FBI."

At lunchtime, Lisa took Mikhail home and hid him in the attic. "Relax," she told him. "We're always having speakers in to talk about their jobs. A couple months ago it was an airline pilot. Before that it was a TV reporter. This is just more of the same. I'll tell you all about it when I get home."

But after school, when Lisa came to see him, Mikhail didn't like the look on her face.

"What's wrong?" he asked, alarmed.

"It's not good," Lisa said. She dumped her books on the table and sat down on the couch beside him. "At first the FBI agent talked about how they have a Ten Most Wanted list and how they fingerprint people and catch crooks and stuff like that, but then he started taking questions."

"Uh oh."

"One of the boys asked him about the FBI being called in to hunt for the kidnapped Russian boy. Apparently, things are heating up in Washington. The Americans are denying you've been kidnapped, but to mollify the Russians, they've asked the FBI to look for you."

Mikhail jumped to his feet. "Lisa, I've got to get out of here! Your teacher or one of the students will report that they saw me with you in class this morning, and the FBI will search the attic!"

Lisa tugged on his arm. "Sit down, Ivan, and relax. Cool it. Nobody knows what you look like. All the FBI has is a description that fits millions of kids in this country. Besides, the kids in my class think you're my cousin, remember? Your accent really isn't noticeable, so there's no reason why anyone would think you are the missing Russian." Lisa went over to the table, opened her book bag, and pulled out a portable radio.

"This is Scott's," she said. "He won't mind if you borrow it. The national news comes on TV at 6:30. We don't have a spare TV, but on this radio, real low on the FM band, you can pick up one of the TV networks." She pointed to the dial. "I've already got it set. At 6:30 just turn it on, and you can hear the TV news. Perhaps there will be a story about you. Before we panic and decide what to do next, we ought to listen and find out what's going on. Perhaps it's all exaggerated. I mean, you ran away from a Cincinnati amusement part. Who would think to look for you in the garage attic of a suburban Columbus home?"

Mikhail smiled weakly and took the radio from her. "I suppose you're right," he said.

Chapter Eleven

His was the third story on the national news that night. He sat on the couch, his stomach twisting into knots, and heard his disappearance described as "the latest threat to detente." Until now, the announcer said, some officials suspected his disappearance was a fabrication by the Russians, an excuse to avoid the upcoming summit between the American president and the Russian premier. Others claimed the story was a fake planted by right-wing Americans who didn't want the president sitting down at peace talks with the premier. But now, for the first time, the Russians were releasing the boy's name and photograph. The president asked the FBI to find Mikhail, and the FBI had asked the Ohio Highway Patrol to keep their eyes open, in case Mikhail was still in the state.

As soon as the story ended, Scott came upstairs, followed by Lisa.

Scott shook his head. "The fat's in the fire now," he observed ruefully. "Good thing Ben was working late. He missed the news and didn't see your picture, or he'd be asking a lot of embarrassing questions."

Lisa deposited his dinner on the table and glared at Mikhail. "You lied to us," she charged. "You said your name was Ivan Petrovich Belkin!"

"Oh, for heaven's sake, Lisa!" Scott snapped. "What difference does a name make? John Peter is our friend and he's in a jam! Don't be so petty!"

"His name isn't John Peter," Lisa said sulkily.

Mikhail said seriously, "I am sorry I lied about my name, but I was afraid, you see." He looked at the plate. "Your mother, too, will get suspicious with all this food missing."

"No she won't. What's a couple of chicken legs? She'll think Scott ate it. He has a big appetite these days."

"Thanks," Scott said dryly.

"Imagine a country with so much food, you don't notice when it's missing," Mikhail marveled. Then he froze, remembering what had happened earlier in the day.

"What now?" Scott asked.

"My picture was on TV," Mikhail whispered. "And I went to school with Lisa today. Everybody there saw my face."

"Oh, no," groaned Scott. "Now we've got to hope no one calls the authorities before tomorrow. We'll smuggle you to Granddad's farm. No one will think of looking there."

"But what if someone does come here tonight asking questions?" Mikhail persisted.

"No sense borrowing trouble," Scott said. He slapped Mikhail on the back good-naturedly. "Look at it this way, John Peter. It's not every kid who gets to be the center of an international incident."

Mikhail gave him an appraising look and turned to watch Lisa. "What are you doing?"

Lisa was poking her head between two garment bags and fishing around for something. Her voice sounded muffled. "I'm hunting for a little . . . there it is!" She pulled her head out and her arms followed. In them was a small pink suitcase with Strawberry Shortcake on the side. She brought it over for his inspection. Inside were a number of dolls.

"My international doll collection. I really don't play with them any more, so I put them in here so they don't get dirty. I have dolls from Scotland, Thailand, and Israel. Granddad travels a lot, so he brings me dolls from wherever he goes." She pulled them out one by one and stacked them on the floor. "Here's the doll from France, and China, and Italy, and Mexico. Mom also used to give me a doll for each birthday."

"You don't have one from Russia," Mikhail observed.

"No," Lisa said. "What sort of costume do they wear?"

Mikhail shook his head. "It's not the costume.

It's the doll itself that is different. They stack, one inside the other."

"You're kidding!"

"I am not. Each doll is a series of smaller dolls. But why are you getting your dolls out?"

Lisa got up and walked over to the open trunk. "It's not the dolls I want, it's the suitcase." She leaned over the trunk and brought out several shirts, slacks, and a sweater. "For you."

Mikhail was astounded. "For me? What would I want with a pink suitcase with a little doll painted on the side?"

"For clothes. You can't stay in those the whole time we're at Granddad's farm."

"You're not going to put them in that little suit-case! I'm not going to carry a suitcase like that! Do you think I'm a sissy?"

Lisa knelt down and began to fold the clothes neatly into the open suitcase.

"Of course not," she said. "You won't carry it. I will. Both Mom and Granddad know I keep my dolls in here. If I take it in the car, they'll just think I'm taking my doll collection with me to the farm. Besides, like I said, you need a couple of changes of clothes."

He reached out and gave her shoulder a squeeze. "You are a very smart girl, and I thank you."

Lisa looked up, startled, and glanced at

Mikhail's hand still on her shoulder. She blushed. He hastily dropped his hand. He could feel blood rushing to his face, too. "I will help you," he said.

Less than half an hour after Lisa and Scott left, Mikhail heard a car pull up in front of the house. He snapped off the flashlight he had been using to look through magazines and peeked out the window. In the twilight he saw two tall, dark-haired men coming up the walk. Cautiously, he opened the window a crack to listen.

"Ruth Meyer?" one man asked when she answered the door.

"Yes," she said.

"My name is Andrews. This is my partner, Don Hendricks. We're from the FBI." He showed her a folding leather case. From the gleam of the porch light, Mikhail could see a shiny badge. "We'd like to talk to you."

"Come in," she said, and the men disappeared inside.

Frantically, Mikhail pulled off his shoes and hid them in a trunk. He had to be quiet. He stuffed the dinner dishes and remains of his meal under a sofa cushion, then slipped the magazine backed into its dusty pile. What if the FBI came upstairs and found him? He couldn't let that happen. But there was no way out of the attic except through the garage, and if he tried to sneak out now, surely one of the FBI agents would hear him and capture him. Would they torture him? Would they turn him over to the Russians at the consulate and let the KGB torture him? He didn't know what the official policy was toward twelve-year-old defectors, but Mikhail didn't intend to find out. He had to hide.

The sofa was too low to hide under, and the garment bags and boxes in the corner wouldn't shield him from view for long. Then his eyes fell on the trunks. As quietly as possible, he lifted the lid. No squeak. Good. He shoved a handful of clothes aside, climbed in, then cautiously lowered the lid. The dimness of the attic faded to pitch blackness. He burrowed as deeply under the clothes as he dared, then tried to cover himself completely. It wasn't a perfect disguise, but he had to hope it was good enough. He also had to hope he wouldn't suffocate. The clothes smelled of moth balls. Now all he could do was wait. And waiting was always the hardest part.

He must have fallen asleep. The next thing he knew, someone was walking around in the attic. Through a crack in the trunk, Mikhail could make out a sliver of light. The light seemed to move in and out of his field of vision. The footsteps sounded closer, then further away, then closer again as the searcher combed the attic. He heard a squeak. It was the lid on the other trunk being lifted. The lid was lowered. The footsteps came nearer.

Mikhail squeezed his eyes shut. There was a flood of light and a gust of fresher air as the searcher lifted the lid on his trunk.

A hand pulled some clothes off his head. "You can come out now," said a familiar voice.

Chapter Twelve

Mikhail opened his eyes and sat up to see Scott grinning at him.

"Did you wet your pants with worry?" Scott asked.

Mikhail signed in relief. "I thought you were one of those FBI men," he said.

"I know. Here. Give me your hand and I'll help you out. That's better. You okay?"

"My nose is full of moth balls."

"I'll bet," Scott said sympathetically. "Sorry I couldn't get up here sooner, but I wanted to make sure everyone was asleep."

"What time is it?"

"A little after two in the morning."

Mikhail rubbed his back, stretched, then sat on the sofa. "What happened?"

Scott shook his head. "Sheer bad luck. One of the FBI agents was a guest speaker in Lisa's class this afternoon. After class, one of the kids went up to him and mentioned that Lisa's friend looked a lot like the missing boy from the Russian consulate, and the kid asked the agent how they traced missing kids. Well, the agent answered the bit about tracking down missing kids, but I guess he didn't seriously consider the bit about you being with Lisa until later. So after dinner he and his partner came to check it out. Lisa told them you were a new kid at school, then Mom put in that you didn't look much like that picture on TV and that your father was very nice."

"But she's never met my father!" Mikhail exclaimed.

Scott laughed. "Crazy, isn't it? But your manners are so nice, and you and Lisa apparently have talked about your dad enough that Mom *feels* as if she's met him. I think the agents got the idea that she had. Not that Mom would lie, that's what's so goofy about this whole thing. They just didn't press her on this. When Ben told them you'd been over for Sedar and didn't have a Russian accent, that clenched it. He wouldn't lie either, and you could just see the FBI guys making the assumption that John Peter Belkin is Jewish, and since *you* aren't, they rapidly lost interest in questioning us further. They just said sorry to bother us and left."

Mikhail looked at Scott for a moment in silence, then shook his head. "Amazing," he said.

Scott shrugged. "I guess cops in real life aren't always like cops on TV. Some are smart, some are dumb, and lots of others are in between. They hear what they want to hear, or what they *assume* they're supposed to hear, not what someone is really saying."

"I can't stay here," Mikhail said. "I've got to leave."

"And you will," Scott replied. "In the morning. With Granddad. He'll figure out something. But for now, try to get some sleep."

The next morning when Granddad pulled up in his blue Honda, Mikhail could hear Scott loading suitcases into the trunk. Then he asked his Granddad and his mother to come to his room for a moment because he needed their advice.

"You need *my* advice?" asked Mrs. Meyer in a humorous voice. "My teenage son needs advice from his mother?"

Mikhail couldn't make out Scott's reply, but it sounded embarrassed. He heard the door to the house slam, then with a clank, he watched the stairs unfold into the garage. He looked down. Lisa had hold of the chain.

She gestured and said in a stage whisper, "Hurry up, and bring the suitcase!"

Mikhail snatched the pink suitcase and climbed down the stairs as fast and as quietly as he could.

"No, no, the blanket too!" Lisa hissed before he was halfway down.

He tossed the suitcase into her waiting arms, then scuttled up again and grabbed the edge of the blanket. He had dropped it beside him on the floor. He tossed it down, too, then hurried down after it. He gave the stairs a shove, and sent them back into their resting place. He took the suitcase from Lisa and put it in the trunk of the car next to her suitcase and Scott's.

Lisa peered anxiously back toward the kitchen door. They heard nothing. She opened the rear car door and watched him climb in, onto the floor. She draped the blanket over him and whispered, "Good luck!"

Mikhail heard the car door slam shut,then he heard Lisa's footsteps walk over to the house.

"Yoo hoo," she called. "Are you guys about ready? Let's get this show on the road."

Momentarily Mikhail heard the other three come back.

"Really, Scott," said Mrs. Meyer. "I don't know why you needed my opinion. Of course you're going to take your telescope. You always take it. And you know it fits into the trunk of your grand-father's car."

"What's this pink suitcase?" asked Professor Alexander.

"That's my doll case," Lisa said quickly. "I hope you don't mind if I take it."

"Of course not," said her grandfather.

"You're taking the dolls?" asked Mrs. Meyer. "But you haven't played with them for six months."

101

There was a moment of silence, then the professor said heartily, "If Lisa wants to bring her dolls, why shouldn't she? The dolls haven't been to the farm for a while, Ruth. Put your telescope in, Scott, so I can close this thing and we can get started."

Mikhail tried to make himself as small as possible and hoped no one would look in the back seat. If someone did, he hoped they would think nothing of an old blanket tossed carelessly on the floor.

"I'll sit in back," volunteered Lisa. She climbed in.

Mikhail heard two other car doors open, as Scott and his grandfather got in, too. The professor started the engine.

"Have a good time," called Mrs. Meyer. "I'll see you on Sunday. Don't give Granddad a hard time!"

Mikhail felt the car roll backwards down the driveway, stop, turn, and start up again. He gave a sigh of relief. So far, so good. But how would the professor react when he realized he had a stowaway in the car?

Mikhail found out soon enough. Lisa, Scott, and their grandfather kept up a running conversation for more than an hour, then the professor said, "How about if we make an ice cream stop in Logan?"

"Great idea," said Lisa. "I could use a soda."

The professor laughed. "What could you use, Scott?" he asked.

"A rootbeer float," Scott replied.

"Well, I need a cold drink," said the professor, as he swung the car to the right. It slowed, then stopped. "What could you use, Mr. Belkin?" he asked.

Mikhail thought his heart would stop.

"What?" gasped Lisa.

"Who?" gulped Scott.

A hand reached over and pulled the blanket from Mikhail. Fearfully, he looked up.

A pair of amused blue eyes beamed back at him. "You can get awfully thirsty riding under a blanket on the car floor," the professor said. "What will it be, a soda, a rootbeer float, or perhaps a double-dip chocolate shake?"

"Uh, oh," groaned Lisa.

"Speak up, boy. I won't bite you. The ice cream is on me. Do you have ice cream sodas in Russia?"

Wordlessly, Mikhail eased onto the seat beside Lisa.

The professor reached between the two front seats and grasped Mikhail's hand. "Let's try those introductions again. I am Daniel Alexander, and you are . . .?"

"Ivan Petrovitch Belkin," mumbled Mikhail.

"Ah," the professor nodded knowingly. "Alexander Pushkin in person."

Mikhail turned scarlet.

"Who?" asked Lisa.

Her grandfather smiled at all three children. "Alexander Pushkin, the greatest Russian writer who ever lived, sort of a Russian Shakespeare. His pen name was Ivan Petrovitch Belkin."

"How did you know?" asked Mikhail.

"I am a former professor, remember? A *literature* professor. Russia has one of the richest literatures in the world. Another great Russian writer was a fellow named Lermantov. That wouldn't happen to be your real name, would it?"

"You saw his picture on the news!" Scott exclaimed.

Mikhail hung his head and bit his lip. He was upset enough to feel his eyes sting with tears. He didn't want Lisa and Scott to see. Especially not Lisa.

"You can trust me, Mikhail," the Professor said quietly.

At that, Mikhail looked up. "I wanted to from the first," he said. "It's just that when I met you, I didn't know if you would turn me in to the FBI or the CIA. I thought if I used a fake name, and you turned me in, at least I might have a chance to escape."

"No one is going to turn you in, son, if you don't want us to. You are Mikhail Lermantov?"

104

Mikhail nodded. "How did you know? From television?"

"Partly. I also read the papers. The Cincinnati *Enquirer* carried a story, saying you had disappeared from King's Island. I knew Lisa and Scott had gone to King's Island that day. When I saw you at Sedar and you mentioned I looked like Father Frost, then I was sure." Granddad turned to Lisa. "Father Frost is the Russian Santa Claus," he explained. He turned back to Mikhail. "I decided if you wanted to keep everything a secret, well, I wouldn't ruin it." The blue eyes were very kind. "But I *do* want to know what's going on."

Mikhail sighed. "Okay," he said.

"First, however," the professor interrupted, "I suggest we get some ice cream. Mikhail, I'll bet you're the type who just loves chocolate sodas."

"I have never had one."

"Aha, I knew it!" The professor turned the key and the engine roared to life. He eased the car back on the road and sped up as they drove into town. "Well, son, you're in for a treat."

Chapter Thirteen

They sipped their sodas and floats in the car while Mikhail told his story. When he was in the middle of his talk, he suddenly exclaimed, "Hey, can we eat this soda?"

"What do you mean?" asked Scott. "Don't you like it? You're almost finished."

"Oh, it is most delicious," Mikhail assured him. "It's just that it's Passover. Is ice cream a forbidden food?"

"If you keep a kosher Pesach it is," the grandfather replied. "But ice cream itself has nothing in it that is forbidden by the dietary laws. However, if you were an Orthodox or Conservative Jew, you probably wouldn't eat ice cream during Passover unless it was from a box marked 'Kosher for Passover,' which means it was packed under strict conditions and blessed by a rabbi. But we are Reform Jews. We don't eat bread, grains, or leavening, but we have no objections to regular ice cream. We also ride in cars on the Sabbath, and turn lights on and off, and cook, and sometimes don't go to Temple as regularly as we should, but we are still Jews and follow the teachings of the patriarchs and the ethical precepts of Judaism."

"I thought Jews were Jews," Mikhail said.

"There are three main branches of Judaism," the professor said. "But one of the grand things about our religion is its ability to accommodate itself to the times. It changes with the centuries, but the ethics remain the same."

Mikhail frowned. "I am trying to understand," he said, "but it's a little confusing."

"For instance," said the professor, "there is the *Kaddish.* It is a special prayer we say in memory of our loved ones who have died. We say it on the anniversary of their deaths."

"My mother died almost seven years ago," Mikhail said. "So if I were Jewish I would say that prayer for her on the day she died?"

"Right," said the professor. "If you were Orthodox or Conservative, you'd stand up, while everybody else sat and listened, and you'd say the prayer with the rabbi. and whoever else happened to be in mourning. But if you're a Reform Jew, everybody in the synagogue stands and says that prayer together."

"Why?" asked Lisa. "I never did know that."

"Because of the six million Jews who died in the Second World War," her grandfather replied. "Whole families were wiped out by Hitler and his devils. There was no one to say *Kaddish* for them. The *Torah* says in Leviticus that we are our brother's keeper. We must care for one another, help

107

each other. So we take on the dead six million as our own families. We all stand and say the prayer for them, because they have no one else to mourn and remember."

Scott nodded. "So the Jewish religion changes to fit the needs of the time, but the moral principles remain the same."

"Exactly," replied his grandfather. He cleared his throat. "At the moment, Mikhail, I seem to be your keeper. Does your father know what happened to you?"

"No," Mikhail said. "I didn't tell him I planned to run away. I didn't think much about it. I just thought I didn't want to go back to Moscow. I love Russia, but I love America, too. The two men from the embassy took me to King's Island to amuse me and get me out of the way during preparations for the opening of the consulate. That is when I just took advantage of my opportunity."

"Your English is remarkable," the professor said.

"Thank you, Professor Alexander."

"For the moment, call me 'Granddad' like Lisa and Scott do. And for the moment, we'll call you John Peter. But I really think you ought to call your father and let him know you're all right. He must be worried sick."

Mikhail was silent.

"Wouldn't you be, in his place?" Granddad

demanded.

Reluctantly, Mikhail nodded. "But I'm afraid if I call him, the KGB agents will chase me down and punish me!"

Scott pointed. "You can call from that pay phone. Stay on the line just two minutes. I think I read somewhere it takes three minutes to trace a call. Reverse the charges. Just tell them who you are, and who you are calling, and after you tell your father you are okay, hang up."

When Mikhail dialed the number, an operator answered. He told her he was calling collect for Petrov Pavelovitch Lermantov. Hesitantly he gave her his name. It seemed a long time before his father came on the line.

"Who is this?" he asked gruffly in Russian. "I warn you, a joke will not be tolerated."

"Father?" he said in Russian. "It's me, Mikhail."

"Mikhail! Where are you? What have the kidnappers done with you? Are they CIA? Are they hooligans demanding money? Are you all right?"

"I'm fine, Father. I haven't seen the CIA and no one has kidnapped me. I've run away. I . . . I don't want to go back to Moscow." He studied the scarred telephone dial without seeing it.

"I don't understand," his father said plaintively. "Mikhail Petrovitch, are they making you say this at gunpoint? Cough once if they are."

"I'm not going to cough, Father. Really, I'm fine.

I just don't want you to worry. Please don't worry."

"Mikhail, who is doing this to you? Have you been brainwashed?"

"Father, please listen. I am not brainwashed. I am not a prisoner. I just don't want to go home. I want to stay here."

"Why? What has happened?"

Mikhail could feel the tears start and was powerless to stop them. "Listen, Father, I love the New York Mets, the chocolate chip cookies, big ones, and ice cream sodas. You can't get them in Russia. I want to try a hot dog. I don't want to harvest wheat. I'll miss you, Father, I'll miss you a whole lot. But we never really got to spend time together, did we? You were too busy. You never took me to a baseball game. I love baseball, Father. You never took me to a gymnastics meet. I love gymnastics; did you know that, Father?"

"Mikhail, you're raving. Ice cream, wheat harvests, baseball. Are you ill?" His father was starting to sound worried. "Do you want me to take you to a gymnastics meet? Is that what you want? I'll get some tickets as soon as we get back to Moscow."

Mikhail couldn't hold back the sobs. "I'm twelve years old," he said. "If I were Jewish, I would have a bar mitzvah next year. When boys are thirteen, Lisa told me they have this ceremony and they become men. Not because they're all grown up, but because they take a moral responsibility for their own actions. It's a year early and I'm not Jewish, but I guess this is my bar mitzvah, Father."

"Mikhail Petrovitch, have Jewish extremists kidnapped you? Are you in the hands of the Israelis?" He sounded desperate now.

"Father, *please . . .*"

"Mikhail Petrovitch, you're all I have." His father's voice broke.

"I love you, Father." Mikhail said, and hung up the phone. He struggled for a moment to get his sobs under control, then he wiped his eyes on his sleeve. His nose was running. He hated that his nose ran when he cried. He hadn't cried in years. When was the last time? When his mother died? But he was doing this because he wanted to, wasn't he? Well, wasn't he? No one was forcing him. A small voice inside told him that no one would send him to Siberia if they caught him. He wasn't important enough to exile. But if he stayed here, would his father be punished? Despite *glasnost*, would his father face internal exile? No *dacha* near Moscow, but a hovel near Tashkent? Mikhail felt a strong arm come around his shoulders.

"Take it easy, son," said a gruff voice. "Old Father Frost won't let anything happen to you." Then Granddad hugged him tight.

Mikhail felt a handkerchief pressed into his hand.

"Blow."

Obediently, Mikhail blew his nose, then wiped his eyes. "I don't want Lisa to see me," he muttered.

"No problem. Lisa and Scott are in the car. They can't see anything. Listen, son, do you want to go home?"

Mikhail gulped and looked up at the kindly face, framed in wrinkles. "I don't know," he said.

"Tell you what. How about if we spend a day or two at my farm and think things through? I've always found that the peace and quiet by my old fishing pond does wonders for contemplation."

His arm still around Mikhail, Granddad guided him back to the car.

"You were on the phone too long," said Scott accusingly when they reached the car. "People might have traced the call."

Granddad was unperturbed. "No problem. We're leaving at once for the farm. Fasten your seat belts, gang. We'll be there in twenty minutes."

Chapter Fourteen

They drove deep into the Hocking Hills. Much of the land was part of a national forest. The rolling hills were covered so thickly with trees that at times it was impossible to see the land they grew on. Small green leaves were uncurling in the spring breeze, and here and there Mikhail could see patches of delicate wildflowers.

They drove from a wide highway to a narrower one, and then followed small country roads as they wound through the hills. Cows mooed at them, and horses with their newborn foals cantered away as the car passed. Farmers sowed their fields with seed or readied them for the sowing. Housewives pinned up the family's laundry on clothes lines strung between trees. Mikhail felt himself relax as he watched scenic rural America go by.

At last they turned up a gravel road and crunched along on the stones until they reached an old white farmhouse with a sagging porch.

"We have to stop first at Henry Adams' place," Granddad said. "He's been feeding the horses and dog for me. He's also been collecting my mail."

When Granddad stopped the car, a mongrel

dog ran yapping over to them.

"This is Old Bullitt," Granddad said. scratching the dog's head. "He's my buddy."

The dog's tail began to wag frantically, and Old Bullitt rubbed his head against Granddad's legs.

"What's all the noise about, you mangy cur?" growled a voice from inside the screen door. The door opened and a tall, skinny man in faded overalls and a red flannel shirt stepped out.

"Hey there, Daniel," he called. He raised his hand in greeting and thumped his way down the front steps to the driveway. Old Bullitt joyfully circled both his master and the professor in a frenzy of delight.

The farmer raised his hand as if to strike him. "Bah," he rasped. "You calm down, you hear me? If you don't I'll whip you."

Lisa giggled and told Mikhail, "Mr. Adams has never whipped Old Bullitt in his life. It's just an act. He babies him shamelessly."

The dog bounced over to the car, leaped at the door, and barked. Mikhail drew back.

"Don't worry," said Scott. "That old dog is nothing but woof and wag. He'd curl up in your lap if you'd let him." Then Scott raised his voice and opened the door. "Hey, Old Bullitt, do you need a scratch?"

The dog lowered his neck and rolled his eyes in pleasure as Scott scratched him behind the ears.

"You got the grandkids, I see," Henry Adams observed. He ducked his head and peered in the window. "And an extra."

Granddad smiled at Mikhail. "A very welcome extra, too. How are the animals, Henry?"

"Oh, right as rain; couldn't be better. The horses are ready for a good run, and the dog pined for you but ate every scrap of his dinner. Come on in the house; I got your mail. Hey there, kids, you treat your grandpa right, you hear?"

As Henry Adams stomped up the steps, favoring a leg with an old injury, Mikhail heard him say, "Well, Daniel, how was your holiday? Did you eat too much again?"

Granddad's house was only a few minutes from the Adams place. Mikhail couldn't see the farmhouse from the road. A thick cluster of pine trees lined the road on either side of the drive. The drive curved around a pond with a small dock and passed more trees, ending at an old barn. Granddad got out of the car, opened the barn door, then drove the car inside.

"I use the old barn as a garage," he explained to Mikhail. "I store odds and ends here. Hop out, gang. Grab your suitcases. I think I hear Duffy."

Mikhail helped Scott and Lisa bring the suitcases to the house. He heard a high-pitched, pleading bark coming from the red-painted house. The barking became more excited as Granddad put the key in the lock and turned it. When he shoved open the door, a flying fur ball leaped for his chest. Granddad dropped a suitcase and hugged the dog.

"Did you miss me, Duffy? You did? Well, I missed you, too. Look here, I brought you company."

Scott and Lisa stroked the dog, who calmed down as they touched him. Lisa turned to Mikhail.

"This is Duffy. He's a fox terrier. He won't hurt you. Want to pet him?"

Hesitantly, Mikhail reached out a hand. Before he could touch the dog's head, Duffy's nose came up, his tongue darted out, and he covered Mikhail's hand with kisses.

"Duffy likes me!" he said in delight. Duffy gave a woof and a wriggle and snuggled against him.

"Looks like you've made a friend," Granddad said. "Come on upstairs. Mikhail, you can share Scott's room. That is, unless you'd prefer sleeping in the attic."

"Granddad, you knew all the time!" Lisa exclaimed. "How did you know?"

"Let's just say these old eyes don't miss much. Put on your jeans. The horses need exercise."

Mikhail never had been that close to horses. He had seen them on television and in fields, but he had never touched one before. Granddad owned two of them. One was chocolate brown with large, docile eyes. The other was something out of a storybook.

"A golden horse!" he exclaimed.

"A palomino," Scott corrected. "Isn't he a beauty? Want to ride him?"

Mikhail hesitated. The horse looked so big.

"You two ruffians go ahead," Granddad said. "John Peter will stay here with me and Duffy for awhile."

Scott and Lisa saddled the horses, then put on the bit and bridle. They led the horses out of the stable behind the old barn and mounted them. The horses snorted and tossed their heads. They were eager to be off.

"I'll race you to the oak tree," Lisa shouted at Scott.

"You're on!" Scott replied.

Granddad hollered from the stable door. "Make sure you walk them back! I want those horses cooled down before they're stabled again!"

"Granddad, count us down," Scott shouted. He was on the palomino, who tossed his white mane and twitched his tail impatiently.

"On your mark!" Lisa and Scott lined up parallel to each other. "Get set!" They leaned forward in anticipation. "Go!" Both horses took off across the wide green field toward a lone oak at the far end.

Mikhail could hear Lisa and Scott's laughter

blown back with the wind. They reached the tree at the same time, then slowed to a canter and began to circle the field.

"You know," said Granddad, "my grandpa came from Russia. His father used to be a blacksmith on the Ukraine. He must have been a pretty darn good one, because the Cossacks would come to his smithy to have their horses shod."

"The Cossacks," Mikhail repeated, impressed. They were legendary horsemen.

"That's right. Half the time he never knew if those Cossacks were soldiers or robbers. But they all needed fast horses. Sometimes to pay him, instead of a kopeck or two, they'd throw the blacksmith a jewel. He could only guess to whom it had belonged. Probably some nobleman, or even a prince. He never knew if his customers had earned it or stolen it." Granddad shook his head.

"What happened to the jewels?" Mikhail asked.

"He sold them for food. Most people were very poor then." He shaded his eyes against the sun and studied his grandchildren on the horses. "They both have a good seat," he said absently. Then he turned to Mikhail and smiled, "How about if we see what sort of seat you have?"

The brown horse proved to be very gentle once Lisa had nearly worn her out riding her across Granddad's field. The horse stood patiently while Mikhail was boosted into the saddle. Granddad

118

sat astride the palomino and talked to Mikhail constantly.

"Heels down, son. That's right. Now squeeze with your knees. I know it's tough through a big Western saddle, but try. You're getting the hang of it. Ease up a bit on the reins. Relax. You're doing fine. Now gently, kick the horse. She won't buck you off. It's how you tell her you're ready to go. That's right, easy does it. That's a nice, easy walk. How're you doing, John Peter?"

"This is fun!" he said.

He and Granddad walked their horses to the end of the field with Duffy tagging at their heels. Then Granddad asked Mikhail if he was ready for something with a little more bounce. They trotted the horses back to the stable. By the time they got back, Mikhail was grinning broadly.

Scott and Lisa showed him how to curry the horses, so they wouldn't be lathered in sweat, catch cold, and get sick. The animals calmly munched on bales of hay in their stalls while the children groomed them.

"Showers all around," Granddad decreed when they came back into the house. "Then lunch. Then we'll catch dinner. Ever been fishing, John Peter? No? Well, you're in for a treat. I've got some new lures I'll let you try out."

"I'm having a wonderful time," Mikhail told Lisa as they headed upstairs. "The best time in my whole life. But when does your grandfather plant his crops?"

"He doesn't," Lisa said. "A neighbor does. Granddad bought this farm about fifteen years ago. He owns fifty acres and leases most of it to a farmer. The farmer plants corn and soybeans. Granddad raises horses, plays with Duffy, and works on textbooks. He has a big desk in the living room and spreads all his work out there. Sometimes he goes to New York to meet with publishers, but mostly he stays here and works. He goes into Logan once a week for supplies, and if he's snowed in during the winter, he doesn't mind. He works on his books, cares for the animals, and has a wonderful time."

Mikhail looked out the second story window. The farm lay cupped in a little valley, surrounded by forested hills. If he leaned out slightly, he could see the edge of the pond glinting in the sunlight. He took a deep breath. The air smelled sweet, and from someplace nearby, birds sang.

"Hey there!" Scott called.

Mikhail started to turn and got hit in the face with a fluffy towel. He pulled it down and laughed.

"If you don't shower after riding, Granddad with personally dunk you in the pond with the fish."

Chapter Fifteen

An hour later everyone was cleaned up and fed. They were sitting on the small wooden dock, dangling their feet in the water of the pond.

"Too cold," Lisa complained when she first stuck her toes in.

"You'll get used to it," Scott told her.

Granddad tied the new lures to the fishing lines and showed Lisa and Mikhail how to cast. Lisa had done it before but had forgotten how to snap her wrist to sent the line with lure, bait, and sinker shooting out over the pond, only to vanish in quiet ripples below the surface. Mikhail caught on at once.

"Nice cast," Scott approved, and Mikhail felt a warm glow at the compliment.

The warmth increased when Mikhail caught the first fish, a silvery gray, wriggling trout.

"That's a beauty!" Lisa admired.

Granddad helped Mikhail reel in the line, and Scott leaned out over the water with a net, all set to capture the fish.

Granddad dumped the fish in a styrofoam ice chest and said to Mikhail, "Son, you're a natural-born fisherman."

Scott caught one and Granddad and Mikhail both pulled in three glistening trout. Lisa quit in disgust after she lost several that took her bait but slipped off the hook. Much of the time they just sat on the dock in serene silence.

Mikhail listened to the squirrels chattering in the nearby woods and the fish plopping in the pond. He watched the breeze ruffle the new leaves and the sun slip lower on the horizon.

Scott went inside to get jackets. Granddad pulled out a knife and began to clean the fish, showing Mikhail how to filet them. It was messy work, but Mikhail didn't mind.

"You know, Granddad, this is the best day of my whole life," Mikhail said.

Granddad smiled. "Well, you've had a lot of firsts today."

Mikhail nodded. "My first soda, my first trip to an American farm, my first ride on a horse, and my first fish." He scraped scales a moment in silence. "It is so very beautiful here. I remember once, when I was little, my parents took me to the Black Sea, to Sevastopol. It was a long train trip. I had no idea Russia was so big. When I told my father, he laughed and said I was seeing only the tiniest part of it. I'd always wanted to go to the Ural Mountains. I hear the country is beautiful there. The only mountains I have seen I have been by plane, and then they don't look like so much, just little folds in the land. But this place," Mikhail paused and looked around, drinking in the sights and sounds, "it is so peaceful, it must be as beautiful as the Urals. I wish my father were here to share it with me."

Granddad fileted a fish and placed it aside. Duffy padded over to sniff it, and Granddad shoved him away. The dog sighed and sat down beside Mikhail. Granddad reached for another fish, then said, "Are you close to your father?"

Mikhail shrugged. "Not really. He is always so busy. He has a very important job with the embassy, or rather, he *had*. I was so sure he was going to be named consul in Cincinnati. I was so *sure* . . ." Mikhail bit his lip. He looked down and scraped fiercely.

Granddad took the fish from his hands and put another in its place. "Easy does it, boy. You want to leave a little something for the dinner table."

"It's funny," Mikhail continued as if he hadn't heard Granddad, "most of my memories of Russia are a blur. I left there when I was six years old, right after my mother's funeral, so my memories are mixed up with that. But mostly what sticks in my mind are the little things. Like tagging along with my mother, clutching her big overcoat as she shopped at Yeliseyev, a store with food counters and fancy ceilings and the most incredibly beautiful chandeliers that hang upside down, like flowers. Or listening to the clock chime in Spassky Tower. Or passing by St. Anne's Church, a lovely little church on the banks of the Moscow River right beside this huge hotel. It has three onion domes, not as big and fancy as St. Basil's Cathedral, but so graceful. And I remember sledding in Gorky Park with my mother. Did you know that in the winter, park attendants pour water on the paths to freeze them, so you can slide hundreds of yards without stopping?" He fell silent.

"Mikhail Petrovitch Lermantov," asked the old man gently, "do you want to go home?"

He looked into the kindly face with the wise blue eyes and sighed. "I don't know," he said at last. "I think so."

Duffy whimpered and licked him on the ear. Absently, Mikhail scratched his neck. "Your people have been looking for you since you disappeared," Granddad said. "Sunday evening your picture was on the Cincinnati television news. Your people think you were kidnapped."

"That's not true!" Mikhail said fiercely. "I told my father I ran away. The Russians *know* I ran away because they had two men take me to the amusement park, and they chased all over trying to catch me. But I was too fast." He grinned briefly at the memory.

"Why did you run away?"

"Because I didn't want to leave America. I love this country."

"And you love Russia."

Mikhail sighed again. "Confusing isn't it? How can I love both countries and only be allowed to live in one? Whatever I decide, that will determine where I live for the rest of my life. I'm too young to get a job and an apartment here. And I don't know if I could stand being alone in the United States. I wish my father would stay in America, too."

Granddad fileted the last fish and set it beside the others. "If he did," Granddad said, "you still couldn't go sledding in Gorky Park."

"Oh, why can't our two countries be friends? We were friends during World War Two. We worked together when we had to, didn't we? Well, if we could do that in war time, why not in peace time? What happened to the friendship? Why do Russia and America build lots of nuclear weapons and threaten each other?"

Granddad laid an arm across his shoulders. "Mikhail, I have no idea. You ask questions that would baffle the wisest rabbis. I suppose what we have to do is have men and women of good will work for peace. Peace doesn't just happen, especially when two countries are so different in culture and outlook. We have to work for understanding, because only if we understand why people are different will we come to appreciate them.

125

And if we appreciate them, we cannot be ene-mies."

Mikhail shivered.

Granddad stood up and offered Mikhail a hand. "Come on, son. It's getting cold. Let's go in. I'll let you kids whip up a huge salad while I fry some potatoes and fish. Nothing tastes quite as good as fish you've caught yourself."

After dinner, Scott showed Mikhail how to do tricks with the yo-yo. He caught on fast and was delighted to make the yo-yo do what he wanted. Lisa tried her hand at it too, and she also improved. Duffy snapped at the spinning yo-yo, got yelled at, and went to sulk behind the couch. Then Granddad came into the living room.

"Clear night tonight," he observed. "A good night for viewing the stars."

"Oh, Scott, will you set up your telescope, please?" Lisa asked. She turned to Mikhail. "Have you ever looked through a telescope, John Peter?"

Mikhail shook his head. "I have been to the Moscow Planetarium, but it is not the same thing. There, they darken the room and flip on lights that represent stars, then point out the constella-tions to you."

"You're in for a treat," Lisa said. "It's really neat to see the moon close up, and some of the planets. Once we spotted Jupiter and four of its moons."

It took a lot longer for Scott to set up the telescope than Mikhail expected. He fussed over numbered settings, did some math on a piece of paper, then fiddled with something else. Lisa and Mikhail went back in the house and practiced with their yo-yos for about an hour. Then they heard Scott yell.

When they ran out to the back yard, Duffy yapping in excitement, Scott was grinning. "Just take a look through that baby and see what I found!"

Lisa leaned over the eyepiece.

"Careful! Don't jiggle the telescope!" Scott warned.

Lisa gave him an injured look. "I won't. I've looked through your telescope before, remember?" She bent back down, then straightened up and gave a shriek. "Saturn!" she yelled. "You found Saturn! How did you do it?"

Scott laughed. "The astronomy section of the paper last Sunday said it would be visible. So I lined up the coordinates, and there it is."

Can I see?" asked Mikhail eagerly.

"You bet," Scott said. Duffy thumped his tail. He acted like he wanted to see, too.

Lisa moved over to let Mikhail have a chance. The sight made him gasp. There, in perfect miniature, was the planet surrounded by rings. The telescope was only powerful enough to let him make out two of the largest rings. But off to the side he could also see two of the planet's moons.

Granddad had a peek, too. "So it's really there," he teased them. "The astronomers weren't making up stories."

"That's amazing," Mikhail told Scott. "You did a remarkable job picking out Saturn from all the lights in the sky. Without a telescope, all the lights look the same. Even with the coordinates, I am sure I could not have found it. I would not even know which were planets or which were stars."

"Scott is terrific," Lisa said loyally. "He's really good at it. He wants to be an astronomer when he grows up." She turned to her brother. "Now can you show us the moon? John Peter, wait till you see all the craters of the moon! It will knock your socks off."

While Scott obligingly changed the setting and aimed the telescope at the moon, Lisa said, "There is a beautiful moon out tonight. I wonder if on some distant planet, around some far away star, people are looking at us and saying, 'There is a beautiful Earth out tonight.'"

"They wouldn't call it Earth," Mikhail said. "They wouldn't know that word."

"And they won't be people like us," Scott said. "They'd probably look so different, we couldn't imagine them."

"But if they think and dream and look through telescopes, they'd still be people," Lisa insisted.

Granddad nodded. "That's a pretty perceptive thought, Lisa. What makes people human is their ability to reason and appreciate beauty. That's what the old rabbis meant when they said we were created in God's image. Not that we look like Him on the outside, but that we have His qualities on the inside. Yes, if there are people on planets around distant stars, I am sure they would have those qualities."

"They would think we all looked alike," Mikhail chimed in. "They probably wouldn't be able to distinguish different features without practice."

Lisa nodded, "Like some white Americans who say all Orientals look alike, even though that's silly. They don't. Those people just aren't used to looking at different features."

Mikhail added soberly. "And if they couldn't tell us apart physically, they really wouldn't be able to understand our differences mentally. They probably would be astounded to learn that on one tiny world, we can't get along."

"That drives me crazy," Lisa said frankly. "I wish we all could be friends. We all want peace, don't we? No one wants a nuclear war that would wipe out the planet."

"I hope there's a planet left when I grow up," Scott said. "I want to meet those alien people some day."

"You've got to think positive," Granddad said.

"From the beginning of the world, people thought the problems their particular generation faced were insurmountable. But they worked together, and sometimes, more often than not, they ironed them out. When I was a boy, we had a Depression. Lots of people out of work, homeless, and hungry. But we solved that. We faced a terrible enemy, an enemy from the *Sitra Achra*, the other side, the dark side, and we defeated them in World War Two. When you kids grow up, I hope you'll figure out a way to bring us all together in peace. It can be done because it has to be done."

"We'll do it," Mikhail said confidently. "Won't we, Lisa?"

"Yes," she said. "Think of all the kids of the world who want peace. If we all want the same thing, it seems to me it's possible to have it."

"Do you guys want to look at the moon or not?" Scott asked. "You keep up this jabbering, and it will set before you ever look through the telescope."

The next morning, Granddad served them *matzoh brei*, a combination of eggs and softened matzohs scrambled together with a little sugar. Duffy followed the food with a longing look in his eyes. As Granddad dished out breakfast he said, "I have a special surprise for you guys this afternoon. The Reds are playing an exhibition game in Riverfront Stadium. It's for charity. I thought we might make a trip to Cincinnati this afternoon. It's a long trip, but it's supposed to be another nice day. I don't know about you, but I have an itch to watch baseball again."

"Oh, boy!" said Lisa. "Would I ever love to see the Reds play!"

"I could go for that," said Scott with a grin.

Granddad looked at Mikhail, "John Peter?"

Mikhail slowly shook his head. "I can't believe I'd get to see a real, live baseball game! Can I have a hot dog?"

Granddad laughed. "What's a baseball game without a hot dog?"

Scott asked, "Who are the Reds playing?"

"The Mets," Granddad replied.

"The *Mets!*" Mikhail shrieked and jumped up.

Duffy stood up and barked. All three looked at him in astonishment. Mikhail sat down, embarrassed. "Sorry," he apologized. "It's just that the Mets are my favorite team. My first baseball game and I get to see the Mets!"

"That's right," Lisa said. "I remember we talked about it in the attic."

"Tell you what," Granddad said. "I'll even spring for a Mets baseball cap, John Peter."

"Oh, wow!" he exclaimed, like Lisa, and everyone laughed.

"First, though, I'll demand payment," Granddad said with a grin. "I want you to help me do the

131

dishes. Lisa and Scott, you go clean up your rooms. If I know you, the beds are unmade and the pajamas are on the floor."

"Okay," Mikhail agreed. Then he glanced at Lisa out of the corner of his eye and said teasingly, "But in Russia the men never do dishes. The women do. It's women's work."

"Hmm," said Granddad. "I have an American apron that would just about fit a boy your size."

"Women's work," snorted Lisa in disgust.

Before she could reply further, there was a knock at the front door. Duffy growled and charged at the door. Granddad went to answer it, and when he returned, Henry Adams was with him, Duffy trotting happily at their heels.

Henry Adams nodded at the children. "How do, kids," he said. "Having a nice time with your grandpa?"

"Of course," Lisa said. "Granddad's the greatest."

Henry didn't smile. He turned to Granddad instead and said, "I thought I'd better warn you, Daniel."

Granddad looked startled. "Warn me? About what?"

"A bunch of men in overcoats are swarming over the countryside asking a lot of funny questions."

"Questions about what?"

"About a missing boy who they claim's been kidnapped and held in the Ohio hills." He set his mouth grimly. "They say they're detectives, but they sound like Rooshuns to me." He inclined his head toward Mikhail. "They showed a picture of a boy that looks just like him. Your extra," he added with a sour smile. "They came to my farm just a bit ago and asked me if I'd seen him, and I looked them straight in the eye and said, 'Nope.' You're good people, Daniel. I figure if you're hiding that boy from them Rooshuns, there's a good reason. But they're nosing around every holler. It's possible somebody up Logan way might have spotted him with you, and it's only a matter of time till they come knocking on your door. So I brought my truck. You take it and get out. I'll drive your car home and stick it in the barn behind the hay bales. If them Rooshuns are looking for your car they won't find it, and they won't stop a man in a pickup truck with three kids." He glanced up at the big clock on the wall. "So you all better get."

Granddad clapped him on the arm. "Henry, you're a good friend, and I won't forget it." He looked at the silent children. "Hop to, kids. Forget the beds and the dishes. Grab your jackets. We'll leave Duffy here and head out now."

Chapter Sixteen

Moments later, they were bumping along in Henry Adams' old red truck. Mikhail and Lisa sat with Granddad while Scott rode in the back. Mikhail noticed the seat was split and smelled distinctly of Old Bullitt.

"Granddad," Lisa asked after they'd spent some silent minutes traveling from one back road to another, "why did Mr. Adams lie when the Russians asked him about John Peter?"

"Why did you lie to your mother about him?" he asked.

Lisa squirmed uncomfortably. "I didn't *exactly* lie," she said. "I just stretched the truth a little."

"You mean, if she had a mistaken impression, you didn't bother to correct it?"

Lisa nodded. "But I didn't want John Peter to get caught. I mean, he came to me for help. I couldn't turn him in. He hadn't done anything wrong. He just ran away. It's not like he's a criminal or anything."

Granddad seemed satisfied. He steered the truck around a pothole. "It was the same with Henry. You know the old rabbis had a saying, 'Saving one life is like saving the world.' That's because if you save someone's life, you save their unborn children and grandchildren, children who never would have been born if you had let the first person die. You save a whole world of people."

"It's sort of a fancy way of saying that every single person *matters*, right, Granddad?" Mikhail asked.

"You have a wise head, son. That's exactly what it means. Everyone is important."

"So Mr. Adams and I saved John Peter's life?" Lisa asked.

"Well, I doubt they'd hurt him," Granddad said. "You may not have saved him physically, but perhaps you saved him spiritually. His people just want him back, but you and Henry gave him some breathing room to decide his own future."

Mikhail looked out the smeared window at the dusty road winding before them. "So I have to make up my mind, don't I?"

No one answered, but Mikhail took that for a yes. He watched the road for a while in silence, then he said in a low voice, "I suppose I had better go back."

"Only if you want to," Granddad replied. "If you'd prefer, we'd make it possible for you to stay here."

Mikhail looked at him. Granddad's jaw was firmly set. "But it might create trouble for you. Or an international incident."

135

"Bah," Granddad said with a smile. "I can handle trouble. And it's already an international incident."

Lisa stared at her grandfather. "It is?"

"Yup. I saw it on the news. I just didn't tell you kids. The Russians claim the Americans have kidnapped Mikhail. The Americans, of course, say they haven't. They put the FBI on it."

"You're kidding," Mikhail said, shocked.

"Why didn't any of the kids spot him at school with me?" Lisa asked.

"People tend to see what they expect to see," Granddad answered. "They expected to see your cousin, so that's who they saw. They didn't see a kidnapped Russian boy."

"I'd better go back," Mikhail said in a small voice.

"Only if you want to, son."

"I do," he said. "I want to see my dad again. I want to go home."

"Oh, John Peter," Lisa turned to him, and her eyes shone with tears, "do you really? I'll really miss you. I wish you'd stay. You could live with us."

"I'll miss you, too," said Mikhail. "You are my friend, and I will always remember you and your courage in hiding me. Someday I hope I can come back and see you again."

"Oh, Mikhail," Lisa said, using his proper name

for the first time. "Must you go?" She bit her lip, then said, "Will you write to me?"

"If they'll let me," Mikhail replied.

Lisa started to sob. Granddad cleared his throat and said briskly, "Now we have to figure out how to return you to your father. I think I have a plan."

They stopped in a small town for a tuna salad and glass of milk, then kept driving. They got to Cincinnati too early for the game, so Granddad took them to the zoo. None of them enjoyed the animals as much as they might have otherwise. The atmosphere was gloomy.

They got to Riverfront Stadium along the Ohio River shortly before game time. Granddad bought the tickets and a program. He guided them to seats between third base and home plate. The place was beginning to fill up. It was a lovely April day, bright and unusually warm. The playing field was so green, the color seemed to vibrate. The bases looked extra white by comparison. Mikhail looked across the field to the opposite bleachers. They shifted and shimmered with color, every hue of the rainbow, as brightly dressed people made their way to seats. The happy, lively sound of a crowd enjoying itself reminded Mikhail of a trip he had made years ago to the circus in Moscow, and the sound made him feel good again. The excitement was catching.

"Scott and Lisa, save our seats. John Peter, come with me," Granddad said, and stood up. Mikhail stood, too, and followed Granddad along the row to the aisle. They went down countless stairs, then came to the area under the stadium where vendors sold food and souvenirs. Granddad marched up to a souvenir stand.

"We'd like one Mets baseball cap, please," Granddad said, and pulled out money.

"One cap it is," the salesman replied. He leaned across the counter and slipped it firmly on Mikhail's head.

"Thank you," Mikhail said to both the salesman and Granddad. "This cap is wonderful."

"Glad you like it, son," said Granddad. "Every-one of my grandchildren has a baseball cap. Kathy and Amy have Reds' caps, though they don't wear them much anymore. Scott and Lisa also have Reds' caps at home. So I thought my newest grandchild needed one, too." He beamed at Mikhail.

"I would be honored to be your grandchild," Mikhail said softly.

"Come on then, Grandson. We have a job to do."

Mystified, Mikhail followed him through crowds of baseball fans to a telephone booth.

Granddad turned around, his face serious. "Mikhail, if you want to go home, this is your chance. I want you to call your father and tell him you will meet him at gate 3 here at the stadium, during the seventh inning stretch. That's the break in the game when everyone stands up and stretches. It's an old custom started by a former president."

"What if the KGB agents find you and Scott and Lisa?"

"They'll stop looking once you are safe and you tell your father what happened to you. During the seventh inning, you'll go to gate 3 alone. If KGB agents do come, they won't have any idea where you are sitting in the stands until you walk over to your father. Look around, son. There are forty thousand people here today. Could you find one twelve-year-old boy in such a crowd?"

"No," said Mikhail. "That would be impossible."

"See?" asked Granddad, satisfied. "Then when the game ends, Lisa, Scott and I will go back to the farm. And you will go back to your consulate."

Mikhail tried a small smile. It was hard to get out. "Perhaps my father will stay with me until the end of the game. That way, just once, we can watch baseball together."

Granddad put an arm around his shoulder and gave him a squeeze. "That's the spirit," he said. "Now make the call."

After he hung up, Mikhail and Granddad returned to their seats.

The game was everything Mikhail had expected, and more. The score kept see-sawing back and forth between the two teams. The Reds retired two pitchers. The Mets retired one. Eric Davis managed a double for the Reds, and Kal Daniels drove him home. Then the Mets got a three-run homer. The crowd was frequently on its feet cheering, Mikhail included. In the middle of the fifth inning, Granddad bought him his first hot dog. Mikhail decided that there was nothing quite as good as a hot dog during a baseball game. Then he spotted the men in the trench coats.

He nudged Lisa, "Look at that man down there at the end of the aisle, the one in the brown coat. See him?"

Lisa craned her neck. "Where?"

"Over there. More to your right. Beside the woman in the flowered jacket."

"Oh, yes. So?"

"I'll bet money he's a KGB agent."

Lisa turned to him, her dark eyes round. "Really? A Russian secret policeman? Wow! I've never seen one in person before! Hey, Scott!" She poked her brother. "John Peter has spotted a KGB agent."

Scott watched the agent for a moment as he scanned the faces of the crowd. "Naw," he scoffed. "That's not KGB. That's FBI. What do you think, Granddad?"

Granddad studied the man uneasily. "I think you'd better keep your eyes on the game. And you, John Peter, you keep that cap on your head. I doubt he's looking for a grandfather with three kids."

A short time later, Scott spotted a second man studying faces in the crowd. Lisa found a third.

"Wow," Scott murmured. "They're everywhere. What do you think they are, Granddad, KGB or FBI?"

"I think it hardly matters. They're looking for John Peter, whoever they are, and we want to be sure they don't find him before his father does."

Meanwhile, the Reds put the tying man on base. It was Eric Davis again. Kal Daniels, with his powerful bat, walked up to the plate and the crowd was on its feet. One strike. One ball. Two balls. Three balls. A foul tip into the stands. That made the count three and two. The crowd was roaring encouragement.

Granddad leaned over and touched Mikhail on the shoulder. "This is your chance, son. You can slip past those men to your father."

Mikhail searched the kindly, wrinkled face with the clear blue eyes that had reminded him of Father Frost. "Oh, Granddad," he said, "thank you for everything. I'll never forget you." Impulsively, he reached over and hugged him. Strong arms held him tightly for a moment, then released him.

Scott shook his hand gravely, "I hope you know what you're doing, Mikhail."

"I do," Mikhail said confidently.

"Well, take care of that yo-yo. Keep practicing. You'll be the yo-yo champ of Moscow. I'm certain."

It sounded a little dopey, but Mikhail knew Scott found it too difficult to say what he really meant. Lisa didn't. She flung her arms around his neck and gave him a kiss on the cheek.

"Oh, John Peter, or Ivan, or whatever your name is, I'm really going to miss you. The attic won't be the same without you. Please write to me and let me know you're all right. Then come back to visit me someday."

"I will if I can, Lisa," Mikhail promised. He felt a warm glow in his chest. No girl had ever kissed him before. "Perhaps you will visit me. I'll take you sledding in Gorky Park. And you take care of that new baby," he added suddenly. "Babies are pretty nice sometimes. I always wanted a younger brother or sister. Perhaps you can take him to the attic and tell him about me sometime."

"I will, Ivan," she promised. "Please be careful."

Then Daniels hit his second home run of the afternoon. Anyone who hadn't been standing, jumped to his feet, and the taped music began to blare hysterically from the speakers all around the stadium.

"Go on now, son," Granddad said. "Your father

is waiting."

Mikhail made his way down the many stairs to the heart of the stadium, slipping past the watchers in trenchcoats without incident. They couldn't find him in the celebrating mass of people. He stopped by the souvenir stand where Granddad had purchased the cap and looked toward gate 3. His father stood there, hands in his pockets, with a tired and anxious look on his face.

"Papa!" Mikhail shouted.

His father turned and the anxiety vanished, replaced by a look of sheer joy. "Mikhail!" he bellowed.

Then Mikhail ran as fast as he could into the waiting arms of his father. He could not remember when his father had given him a bigger hug. "Oh, Mikhail, I was so worried," he kept murmuring in Russian. Then he released his son and held him at arm's length. "You look fine," he said, "but what in the world is that thing on your head?"

"It's a Mets cap," Mikhail told him happily. "Oh, Papa, do you suppose we could stay and watch the rest of the baseball game together?"

Epilogue

Lisa paused and looked down at the sea of faces in Temple, many of them smiling at her, and felt the butterflies in her stomach quiet down.

She smiled at her family in the first row. Her brother, Scott, was growing so fast these days, she couldn't believe how much he towered over her. He seemed so mature since his acceptance into MIT for the coming fall semester. He was on his way to being an astronomer. Granddad looked wonderful in his new blue suit. He had told Lisa he got the suit in her honor. Ben looked as proud of her as if she were his own daughter. Her mother was positively glowing. Even tiny Elizabeth, in her frilly pink dress, spared her a smile before sticking a chubby fist back in her mouth. Behind them were Aunt Margie and Uncle Jack, their girls, and Ben's brother and his family from Chicago. Her mother's family was there, too. They had flown in from California for the occasion.

Lisa cleared her throat and continued with her speech. "This bat mitzvah is very special for another reason. I share it with a girl named Katya Reich of the Soviet Union. She and her family are refusniks. They have been refused permission to leave the Soviet Union, so Katya is unable to have a bat mitzvah of her own. Through this ceremony of Women's American Ort, Katya is bat mitzvah by proxy, and she will receive a special certificate telling her so." She paused and looked at Scott and Granddad.

"Today is my bat mitzvah. I become an adult in the eyes of the Jewish community. I now assume responsibilities for my own actions. But in a sense, I had my bat mitzvah a year and a half ago, when I hid a runaway Russian boy who needed time to think. He had to decide which country he loved more, the U.S. or the U.S.S.R. It was a tough decision for him, but he decided to go home.

"Two days ago, I received a letter from him, and a little gift. I want to share it with you."

There was utter silence in the sanctuary. Many people looked thunderstruck. Lisa sneaked a peek at the rabbi. He was smiling at her. She began to read.

" 'Dear Lisa, I know you are getting ready for your bat mitzvah. I hope you do well. I am sure you will. I wish I could join you on this special occasion, but of course I cannot. Perhaps one day, when we are both grown up, we can change the world enough so that friends from different cultures will be able to share happy times together in person. I have joined the Young Pioneers and soon will be eligible to join the Communist Party. I will

145

go to university, and I hope to go into the diplomatic service like my father. I have decided that the world needs more diplomats, more ambassadors of good heart who realize there is more that unites us than divides us. I often think of what your Granddad told me: that peace doesn't just happen, we have to work for understanding; we have to learn to appreciate people and enjoy their differences. I have learned that by appreciating people, we can turn potential enemies into friends. I hope you will always be my friend, Lisa. I will always be yours. Let us work for peace together.'" Lisa looked at her Granddad and smiled. He winked back at her.

On her desk at home was the gift from Mikhail. It was a little, hand-painted Russian doll made of wood. When Lisa unscrewed it, she found a second doll inside the first, and a third inside the second, and so on, until six little Russian dolls stood side by side, each a smaller size than the one before. She then put them back together and stood them on her desk under a very special picture. It was clipped from a news magazine. It showed a Russian boy with blond hair boarding a plane in New York. He had paused at the top of the steps, and that was how the photographer had captured him, smiling broadly and waving good-bye with a Mets baseball cap in his hand.